Other Titles
by L. R. Braden

The Magicsmith Series

A Drop of Magic, Book 1

Courting Darkness, Book 2

Faerie Forged, Book 3

Casting Shadows, Book 4

Of Mettle and Magic, Book 5

Chaos Song, Book 6

Lies and Illusion, Book 7

The Rifter Series
(set in the Magicsmith Universe)

Demon Riding Shotgun, Book 1

Personal Demons, Book 2

A Demon Faerie Tale, Book 3

Dancing with a Demon, Book 4

A Demon Faerie Tale

The Rifter Series – Book 3

by

L. R. Braden

Magical Realms Press

Magical Realms Press
PO Box 24
Broomfield, CO 80038

Print ISBN: 978-1-968414-19-1
Ebook ISBN: 978-1-968414-18-4

We love to hear from readers!
Contact us at:
MagicalRealmsPress.com
LRBraden.com

Cover design: Debra Dixon
Interior design: Hank Smith
Photo/Art credits:
Girl (manipulated) © Fokusgood | Dreamstime.com
Alley (manipulated) © Glenda Powers | Dreamstime.com

Dedication

For Connie.

Thanks for having my back.

Chapter 1

Mira

RAIN DRIPPED OFF the fire escape, creating a *pitter-patter* symphony against the dark metal that echoed through the shadowed alley below. Thick air carried the scents of iron, oil, and the musty green moss that seemed to spring from every crack in this oversaturated city. A cold trickle snuck down the collar of Mira's leather jacket. She shivered against the guardrail bars digging into her back. *I am so ready to be done with this rain.* She shifted positions, trying to get some feeling back in her numb ass, but wet denim restricted her movement. She'd been sitting on the fourth-floor landing for over an hour, and there was still no sign of her quarry.

<Maybe they went to a hotel.> The demon's voice rang in Mira's mind, her constant companion.

Mira sighed and tipped her head back. The rain wasn't heavy enough to make her close her eyes, just a constant drizzle that draped like a blanket and seeped to the skin. Dark clouds blocked the stars, creating an abyssal backdrop to the blazing lights of the towering downtown structures beyond the mouth of the alley. Traffic rumbled in a post-workday frenzy, as people hurried to dinner, dates, or whatever activities normal people filled their time with on a Tuesday night. Mira patted the digital camera in its waterproof case. "They'll be here."

Light flared in a window across the alley, as if on cue. Four stories up, two rooms from the end. Mira perked, rising to a crouch. Rusty metal creaked, making her wince. She glanced at the joints anchoring her stakeout platform to crumbling bricks, praying the nineteen-sixties construction didn't choose this moment to prove why fire escapes were no longer put on buildings. The bolts held. No one stirred in the connected apartment. Not that they'd see her even if they looked. Mira wore shadows like a cloak.

Returning her attention across the way, to the smooth gray stone and mirrored windows of the more modern tower, Mira pulled out her camera. Ignoring the large display, she placed her eye to the viewfinder. Silhouettes moved through the distant room as Mira fiddled with the camera's focus. The larger shape resolved into a middle-aged man in a business suit. Antony Scalduzzi. A stockbroker at a big firm. He had a wife and three kids, none of whom knew about the apartment he kept in the city, two blocks from his office.

"What a sleaze," Mira muttered as she zoomed in.

The room's second occupant stepped into view. Standing at barely five feet four inches, she had to get on her tiptoes to wrap her arms around Antony's neck.

Mira snapped a picture. Lisa Dempsky's husband suspected his wife was having an affair, but he didn't want to believe it. Not without proof. So he'd hired a PI. Mira shook her head. Most of the people who hired her didn't want to be right . . . but they usually were. Lisa's husband certainly had been.

Mira snapped a few more pictures as the two swapped spit in front of the window, then Antony closed the curtain.

Oh no you don't. Mira waited long enough for the adulterers to get their clothes off, then sent a thread of magic toward the window. It was delicate work. Mira was usually more of a "blow a hole in the side of the building" kind of gal, but that sort of magic drew attention—something Mira couldn't afford. Not when she was playing host to a demon.

Inch by inch the curtains parted, revealing the bedroom beyond. Luckily, Antony and Lisa had left the lights on.

"What a pair of idiots," Mira mumbled. "They both have spouses, families, homes, lives . . . They're risking it all. For what? A quick screw?" She shook her head.

<They're doing what feels good in the moment. What's wrong with that?>

"Every choice has a consequence." Mira's mind wandered to Ty, her one-night-stand-turned-crime-fighting-partner. "Acting on desire alone can be disastrous."

<So can repressing it, and letting loose is more fun.>

"In the short term, maybe. But I doubt Lisa will think tonight was worth the cost, once I hand her husband these pictures."

Mira snapped photo after photo as the two cheaters tumbled in the sheets. She felt dirty, as if she were the one doing something wrong. These pictures could end a marriage. Maybe two. But that wasn't her fault. She was just doing her job. Even rifters had to eat.

<What's he trying to do with her leg?>

Mira tipped her head sideways and wrinkled her nose. *Maybe he thinks she's made of rubber.*

2

The demon laughed, though the sound didn't enter the wider world until Mira joined in.

The inner pocket of Mira's jacket vibrated. She nearly dropped the camera. Only one person had the number to her cell phone. Only one person even knew the phone existed.

She zipped the camera into its waterproof case. Antony and Lisa were still going at it, but she had plenty of pictures to break her client's heart. Sitting back, she pulled out her phone and smiled at the name on the display.

<Speaking of desires . . .>

Don't start. Mira answered the call. "How's Vegas?"

"Hot." Ty's deep voice carried through the phone and into the Seattle night. "And over. Finally."

Her smile grew. Not long ago, the very idea of working with a partner would have sent Mira running for the hills, but . . . well, Ty wasn't so bad. Unfortunately, their partnership had to be kept on the down-low, so Ty's participation in a PTF agent training retreat had not extended to her. Even though she was usually on the same side as the Paranatural Task Force, working toward similar—if not always identical—goals, she wasn't one of them. So long as she was a rifter—a demon-possessed magic practitioner—she never would be.

"What are you up to?" Ty asked, shaking Mira out of her self-pity. "Staying out of trouble, I hope?"

"I'm earning a paycheck. We can't all rely on a cushy PTF payroll."

<Bitter much?>

Mira rolled her eyes. It was hard not to feel slighted when she was doing basically the same job as a PTF agent, and a hell of a lot better than most of them, but she was stuck living out of a truck and hiding her real identity, lest she be hunted down herself, while people with not even a quarter of her talent got poolside drinks and capture bonuses.

"Are you still in the northwest?"

"Seattle."

"Perfect," Ty said. "Garrett threw a case my way that might be up your alley."

"Oh yeah? What's the draw?"

"A woman who ate her husband."

<Kinda puts the whole cheating spouse thing in perspective,> the demon said. <At least Lisa here just boinked her boss instead of resorting to cannibalism.>

"Rifters aren't the only beings who eat people," said Mira. "Far from it."

"The woman wasn't a rifter," Ty corrected. "She's dead, too. Choked on a finger bone."

The demon chuckled. <Yeah, no way a demon lets their host die from something as stupid as that.>

Mira pinched the bridge of her nose. "Let me get this straight. A human woman ate her husband, then she choked to death on one of his bones?"

"That's right."

"And what part of that screams 'Let's call Mira'?" She glanced through the distant window. Lisa and Antony were still going. "You're probably looking at a nasty hex put on her by some jilted fae lover."

"Maybe, but sowing chaos and spreading fear is certainly a rifter's MO," he said, "and the Johnsons aren't the only casualties involved." Ty's voice hitched, as if he were fighting to hold his temper. "The PTF dispatched a local team to look into the case—one full field agent and one junior agent learning the ropes. The senior agent died yesterday after guzzling half the liquid inventory of a convenience store, including drain cleaner and engine oil."

The *pitter-pat* of raindrops echoed through the alley. A car horn sounded in the distance.

"I'm sorry." Mira couldn't think of anything else to say. It had been barely a year since Ty lost his previous partner on a PTF case. That had been before Mira met him, but she knew that case, and his sense of guilt, still haunted him.

Ty cleared his throat. "The culprit could still be fae, or an unregistered practitioner even, but a jealous lover probably would've stopped with the Johnsons. Even if this case turns out not to be demon related, I could use your help getting to the bottom of it."

The demon stretched in Mira's mind, like a cat getting comfortable in a patch of sunlight. <He totally wants our company.>

He wants to avenge the dead agent, Mira corrected.

"And you'll get paid," Ty added. "More than a PI taking dirty pictures of cheating spouses."

Mira blushed. Her corner of darkness on the fire escape suddenly felt way too exposed.

The demon laughed, drowning Mira's thoughts. <Nailed it in one! So, what do you think? I'm ready for a change of scenery.>

"Fine," Mira said. "Where am I heading?"

"I'm on a flight to Portland in the morning. You can pick me up at the airport at 9:00 a.m."

"What am I, your chauffeur?"

"See you tomorrow."

Mira hung up and rested her forearms against her knees.

<Admit it, you've missed him.>

Mira squinted through the window across the way. It seemed Lisa and Antony had finally run out of steam. *A few nights of carnal pleasure in exchange for the ruin of their existing relationships. I wonder if they'll think it was worth it?*

Tucking the phone back in her pocket, she grabbed the camera case and started her descent. "Let's get these pictures delivered. We're gonna need gas money." The corner of Mira's mouth twitched. "While we're at it, Antony's wife might be interested to know what his long hours at the office actually look like."

<You think we can get paid double for this job?>

"Whether she pays or not, she deserves to know."

<Are you sure you're not just taking out your frustrations on someone who's having more fun than you?>

"We all have to live with the choices we make."

MIRA DRUMMED HER fingers against her steering wheel and studied the pedestrians milling along the sidewalk. Some strode with purpose. Some wandered aimlessly. Some sat on concrete benches, attention fixed to their phones. Cars pulled to the curb, loaded or unloaded passengers and luggage, then pulled away, only to be replaced by others in a never-ending cycle. There were a few larger vehicles, rideshare vans and the like, but nothing so large as the renovated moving truck Mira called home. She garnered more than a few honks and glares as sedans and SUVs were forced to maneuver around her.

Her fingers drummed faster. She didn't like drawing attention. The size of her vehicle was noteworthy enough in a place like this. The fact that it was currently wearing an illusion to look like a refrigerated catering truck made it stand out even more in the arrivals lane. Who picked up a passenger in a catering truck? But the spell to change the illusion was time-consuming and tiring. She had to make all the details just right, and it was delicate work, not something she could have done while driving through the night to make this meetup.

<There he is.>

Mira perked up at the demon's statement, scanning the crowd.

5

Standing just outside one of the many sets of sliding glass doors along the pickup corridor, Ty wore standard-issue black slacks and a white, button-up shirt that contrasted sharply with the deep richness of his skin. His appearance screamed ex-military, from the tidy trim of his goatee and the angle of his shoulders to the perfect polish on his shiny black shoes. Despite the crisp lines of his long tan coat, Mira noticed the slight bulge of his holstered gun. He glanced up and down the row then headed in her direction. He carried a single bag slung over one shoulder. Ty preferred to travel light—only what was necessary, always arranged just so. Mira respected that. *Never hold on to anything you can't afford to lose.*

Ty opened the passenger door and set his bag on the floor but didn't climb in.

"Slide over." He slipped a manila folder out of his pack and waved it like a fan. "I'll drive so you can familiarize yourself with the details of the case."

<Someone's in a rush.>

"Hi, Mira," Mira intoned in a mocking imitation-Ty voice. "It's so nice to see you. Thanks for driving all the way here in time to pick my lazy ass up from the airport."

Ty smiled and set the folder on the passenger seat. "Hello, Mira. It's wonderful to see you. Thanks for coming. Now scoot over." He closed the door and circled the front of the truck.

Mira slid along the bench seat, lifting the folder so she didn't sit on it.

Ty settled in, typed something on his phone, then set it on the dashboard. A woman's artificial voice instructed him to drive forward. Mira glanced at the listed destination as he turned on the engine.

"The city morgue?"

Ty pulled into traffic. "We're scheduled to meet the junior agent there this morning for the official case hand-off and to talk to the coroner. Hopefully they're done with Agent Reyes's autopsy."

Mira cast a sideways glance at Ty. The muscles in his neck and jaw were tight.

<You should say something,> the demon prompted.

Like what?

<Something comforting or encouraging. Something to let him know you understand his pain and you're here for him.>

Mira cleared her throat. "Are you sure you can handle this?"

<Wow,> the demon said. <You are so bad at this.>

Like you'd do any better. All your relationship "experience" comes from watching soap operas.

Ty glanced at her, then returned his focus to the road. "What do you mean?"

"I just . . ." She shifted on her seat and picked at a corner of the folder with her thumbnail. "You know. Agent Reyes. Jamal."

Ty stiffened at the name of his dead partner, tightening his grip on the wheel till his knuckles turned white.

<I don't think this is helping,> the demon observed.

Mira shrugged. "I guess I'm just saying, if you need to talk or anything . . ." She shrugged again.

"Thanks," Ty said. He exhaled, and some of the tension left his shoulders, as if he were making a conscious effort to relax. "I appreciate the offer."

<Is that what that was?>

"But if you really want to make me feel better, just help me catch the bastard who killed Reyes."

Mira nodded. "Deal." She opened the folder on her lap, grateful to end the conversation.

<That was awkward as ass.>

It was your *idea!*

<Yeah, but the execution . . .> Mira felt the mental equivalent of a shudder. <You really need to up your interpersonal game now that you've got someone you plan to talk to more than once then run.>

Rolling her eyes, Mira focused on the case file.

Trish Johnson, forty-seven years old. Cause of death: asphyxiation. Frank Johnson, forty-nine years old. Cause of death: sharp force injury resulting in exsanguination. In the day leading up to their deaths, Frank worked his usual shift at the mechanic's shop where he was employed. Trish, who had the day off from her job as a reference librarian, ran errands. Witnesses and receipts placed her at a grocery store, a bank, and a yoga parlor. Neighbors say they heard shouting shortly after Frank returned home, which is when the police were called.

Mira flipped the page to find the first-on-scene report. The officer who knocked on the Johnsons' door got no response. They announced themself, then proceeded to circle the house while their partner reported to dispatch. Looking in a window, the first officer observed what appeared to be a man on the floor, though only his legs were visible. The second officer called for an ambulance, then joined the first, and they proceeded to force the door. The scene they found in the kitchen was right out of a horror movie, as evidenced by the crime scene photos included in the file.

Even Mira recoiled, and she hunted demons for a living. She was no stranger to gore.

The wife, Trish, looked as though she'd bathed in blood and used it to finger paint the kitchen tiles. Her dull-brown eyes bulged. Her lips had a distinctly bluish tint. The skin on her hands, arms, and face was seared, even blackened in some places. Blisters coated her injured skin. Her dress was charred, burnt through with dozens of holes. The right side of her shoulder-length blond hair ended in short, singed strands. Mira was glad she couldn't smell the scene in the photo. Burnt hair was not nice, and it brought back bad memories.

Chunks of meat littered the inside of the open oven, as well as the area around it. Mira hoped all those chunks came from whatever had been cooking, but they could just as easily have been pieces of Mr. Johnson.

A close-up photo showed the husband also had burns on his hands and arms, though his face was injury-free. Not that Mira could see much of his face under all the blood. The hilt of a carving knife stuck out of the man's chest, but the blade had made its rounds. His blazer and shirt were slashed to rags; the original colors showed only in a handful of places not saturated to near-black by his blood. Exposed ribs glistened wetly under the harsh kitchen lights, and ragged holes cratered his arm like bites out of an apple.

Mira pressed her knuckles against her lips. *This is gruesome.*

<But she wasn't a rifter. Not if she died from choking.>

Is it possible she walked in on a rifter eating her husband, and the demon decided to have some fun?

<Maybe, but that's a lot of food to waste.>

But killing the wife with the husband's bone would throw off the case and play to their sense of chaos.

<So if we *are* looking for a rifter, it's a clever one.>

Damn.

"Did you check for other suspicious activity in the area?" Mira asked.

Ty nodded. "The only red flag was a grocery store cashier who stole money from her own register then ran into traffic, screaming that she was 'finally free,' only to be hit by a bus."

Mira shrugged. "Maybe she was just greedy."

<And stupid,> the demon added.

"Or maybe there's a demon getting their kicks by making people act batshit crazy."

"Wouldn't be the first time," she admitted.

The truck pulled to the curb. Mira glanced out the window. They were parked beside a pale-brick building with inset doors and windows. The structure towered above its neighbors, as if proclaiming dominance over the groveling relics of the past.

Ty cut the engine and twisted to look at her. "Any insights before we head in?"

"Rifter definitely isn't off the table," she said, "but neither is fae. I need more info."

He pointed to the building's glass lobby. "Then let's get to it."

Chapter 2

Ty

TY WAITED UNTIL Mira closed the passenger-side door before letting out a long sigh. She wasn't wrong that this case was going to have him tied up in knots. How could it not, when it hit so close to home? But the job was the job. He couldn't let himself become distracted, either by thoughts of his old partner . . . or his new one.

Red and gold highlights danced through Mira's brown hair as she turned on the sidewalk to look back at him. The single white streak near her left temple that marked the demon's influence stood out like a ribbon of snow on a rocky mountaintop. She smiled, and the expression crinkled her mismatched eyes—one solid brown, the other lighter, almost golden in color. She tipped her head in a "let's go" motion, prompting him to action.

Locking the truck, he circled around to hand her the keys, but as he stepped onto the curb, his foot caught. He stumbled, nearly dropping to one knee, and only saved himself by bracing one hand against the rough concrete.

"Whoa there." Mira grabbed his arm to steady him. "Did you party too hard in Vegas?"

Ty straightened, putting him a head and a half above Mira. A breeze rustled her hair, bringing him the scent of lavender and soap. He inhaled deeply and glanced at her hand, which lingered on his arm. Coughing, he turned to find what had tripped him, breaking the contact. She stepped away.

A piece of bent metal jutted from the side of a storm drain grate. Ty looked down and found a corresponding tear in the soft leather on the side of his shoe. "Damn it! These were practically new. Now I look like a slob."

Mira inspected her own shoes—a pair of well-worn sneakers colored with a variety of stains.

Ty could have slapped himself. Mira was living off the grid, taking odd jobs as a counterfeit PI because there was no legal place for her in the world. Everything she owned was in the back of her truck, and none of it was new.

"Forget it," he said. "They're just shoes." He pulled open the glass door to the building. "Ladies first."

Mira passed within a breath of him, trailing that lavender-soap perfume. He glanced again at his ruined shoe. *I can buy a new pair once this case is over*, he reassured himself, but the blemish made his palms itch with the need to address it.

He followed Mira to the building directory and found the listing for the coroner's office and morgue. *Basement. Big surprise.*

"Why do they always put morgues in basements?" Mira asked. "It's like they're trying to make them as creepy as possible."

Ty smiled at the echo of his thoughts. "I imagine it has more to do with cooling systems and drainage."

Mira glanced at the elevator next to the directory, then at Ty. "Should we take the stairs?"

His smile faltered. He hated being treated like an aberration, but he hated being stuck in small spaces even more. Just the thought of getting in the elevator made his pulse race. "If you don't mind."

Mira shrugged and pulled open the door to the stairwell. She bowed to him with a sweeping gesture. "Gentlemen first."

The stairwell wasn't much better than the elevator would have been, with shallow steps and tight turns. He glanced up at the reinforced beams of the flights above and imagined what it would feel like if it all came crashing down on top of them. Swallowing to get some moisture into his suddenly dry throat, Ty brushed his side, picturing the scars there, and slipped his hand into his pocket. He wrapped his fingers around the smooth river rock he always carried, tracing the groove in one side with his thumbnail. *The past is the past. Stay in the moment.*

Unfortunately, the past and the present seemed disturbingly similar at the moment.

The stairwell fed into a sea foam-green hallway with a pair of double-hinged doors leading to the morgue at the end. Ty had been in plenty of morgues over the course of his career. That didn't make walking into this one any easier. The concrete floor sloped toward a large drain in the middle of the room. The wall opposite the entrance was a grid of square, two-foot freezer doors. Three examination tables—body-sized steel trays on wheels—along with the tools of the coroner's trade lined the wall to the left. Two tables were empty. The nearest held a sheet-covered lump.

Ty swallowed the sour flavor at the back of his throat and tried not to see himself in the young man standing beside that sheeted body. Junior Agent Michael Kelley looked up when Ty and Mira entered. He ran a hand through his unkempt brown hair. Dark circles underscored his bloodshot eyes, one of which bore a purplish bruise that trailed down his cheek. Deep lines accentuated his frown.

"Can I help you?" A middle-aged woman with a pale complexion and gray-blond hair pulled into a tight braid stood up from behind a desk near the entrance. She wore a white lab coat over her street clothes.

"Are you the coroner?" Ty asked.

The woman nodded.

"I'm PTF Agent Ty Williams." He showed the coroner and Agent Kelley his badge. "I'll be taking over the Johnson and Reyes cases."

"Ah." The coroner motioned for them to come farther inside. "We've been expecting you."

"Who's this?" Agent Kelley gestured to Mira.

"A private consultant," Ty said in a tone intended to dissuade additional questions. "What can you tell me about the Johnson case that I couldn't get out of the report?"

Agent Kelley studied Mira a moment longer, obviously curious why Ty had brought in a consultant and what her credentials might be, then folded under Ty's authority. Clearing his throat he said, "Not much. We'd barely started investigating when Daniel . . . when—" His words choked off. He turned away. "Sorry."

Ty fought the lump forming in his own throat. Had he been any more articulate when he'd tried to describe the events leading up to Jamal's death? He doubted it, though he couldn't remember very clearly. Everything after the screaming was a bit of a blur.

Mira turned to the coroner. "What about you?"

The coroner pulled open one of the freezer doors and rolled a sheet-covered tray halfway out. Flipping back the sheet revealed Trish Johnson's corpse, looking just as gruesome as it had in the crime scene photos. Pulling open a second drawer, the coroner flipped back the sheet on Mr. Johnson as well.

"I've verified from the contents of Mrs. Johnson's stomach that she did, in fact, consume a portion of Mr. Johnson, as well as some pot roast and a disturbing amount of raw ground beef. Also, the bite marks on Mr. Johnson's arm and side"—she indicated the injuries—"are a perfect match for Mrs. Johnson's teeth."

Ty's stomach heaved. Even industrial-strength cleaner wasn't enough to entirely mask the smell of decaying meat wafting off the Johnsons.

"Judging by the burn patterns on both victims," the coroner continued, "the most likely scenario is that Mrs. Johnson was eating pot roast directly out of the oven, *while* it was cooking, and her husband pulled her out."

"Where does the ground beef fit into that scenario?" Mira asked. She seemed disturbingly unaffected by the corpses. *She's seen her fair share of death*, Ty reminded himself. *Then again, so have I.*

The coroner shrugged. "Best guess? Before the pot roast. I doubt she would have had time once her husband entered the room. He clearly reached into the oven, as evidenced by these burns on his forearms." She drew their attention to the burns. "After that, they seem to have struggled. Perimortem bruising indicates the wife was forcefully restrained, but she must have broken loose, because she carved up her husband like a Christmas ham."

"Was he dead before . . . ?" Ty indicated the bite marks.

"Mr. Johnson died of massive hemorrhaging from multiple stab wounds. He was most likely dead before she started eating him."

"Thank Heaven for small mercies," Mira muttered. Her right hand rested over her heart, where Ty knew she wore a medallion of Saint Michael—a symbol of her commitment to do good in the world.

"And the finger bone was definitely the cause of death for Mrs. Johnson?" Ty asked.

The coroner nodded. "The intermediate and distal phalanges of Mr. Johnson's right pinky lodged in her throat, cutting off her air supply."

Ty glanced at Mira. "Any other questions?"

She continued to study the bodies for another moment, seeing more with her magic than he ever could. She shook her head.

The coroner covered the Johnsons with their sheets and rolled them back into their drawers.

The three of them approached Agent Kelley and the sheet-covered slab beside him. Ty cleared his throat. "Can you tell us what happened?"

Kelley nodded, straightened his shoulders, and took a deep breath. "Reyes and I went to the Johnson residence yesterday morning. The scene had been cordoned off, so it was pretty much exactly how you saw it in the crime scene photos except that the bodies had been removed. We did a thorough sweep. Reyes tested for residual magic in the kitchen; he didn't find any." Kelley shook his head. "Reyes said he was thirsty. He suggested we stop at a convenience store we'd passed on the way there. We needed gas anyway. Then the plan was to backtrack Mrs. Johnson's path that day, to see if she interacted with any known or suspected fae."

Kelley licked his lips and shifted his weight from foot to foot.

"Take your time," said Ty.

Nodding, Kelley continued. "Reyes went into the shop while I pumped the gas. I heard a shout. When I turned around, I noticed the clerk at the counter waving his arms at something deeper in the building. He was the one shouting. I left the fueling station and went to investigate. Turns out the clerk was shouting at Reyes, who was standing in front of a half-empty cooler chugging sodas, teas, beers, whatever he could get his hands on. The front of his clothes were drenched. There was a puddle around his feet. Bottles, cans, and coins were all over the floor.

"I ran over and grabbed his arm, shouting at him to stop, asking what he was doing." Kelley sighed and looked down at his hands. They were shaking. "He knocked me down. Then he grabbed another bottle, but this one wasn't a drink. It was a jug of washer fluid. When he pushed me, we ended up in the automotive aisle. He picked up oil, radiator fluid . . . it was like he didn't care what he put in his mouth as long as it was a liquid.

"I screamed for the clerk to call 911, then I tackled Reyes. We struggled. We rolled through the puddle, knocked into shelves. Reyes caught me on the side of the head with an ice scraper, and I went down. He snatched the nearest bottle. Drain cleaner. He didn't even hesitate. Just . . . down the hatch. He convulsed. Fell. I crawled over to him. He was still reaching for another bottle. Then he just—" Kelley shook his head, staring at his shoes.

Ty set a hand on the younger man's shoulder. "There's nothing you could have done."

Kelley nodded, though he didn't look convinced. "I did chest compressions, but he was gone well before the ambulance arrived."

Mira indicated the sheeted body. "May we?"

Kelley gave another nod, but he turned away as the coroner pulled back the shroud.

Ty blinked and cleared his throat, willing away the ghostly image of Jamal that momentarily overlay the dead man's features.

Agent Reyes had been a large man. The lines around his eyes indicated plenty of time laughing or smiling, but there was no pleasure in what Ty saw. Chemical burns in the shapes of drips and splashes stained his lips, chin, and neck an angry red. His face was swollen.

Mira pursed her lips and narrowed her eyes, scrutinizing the corpse.

"Did you interact with anyone at the Johnsons' house?" Ty asked. "Neighbors? Pets?"

"No." Kelley answered with his back to them.

"Did Reyes touch anything at the crime scene without his gloves on?"

"Of course not!" Kelley spun to face him, fists balled. "Reyes was an excellent agent."

Ty raised his hands, palms out. "No one is questioning Agent Reyes's competence. But we need to investigate every possible angle if we want to catch whoever did this to him."

Kelley seemed to deflate.

"Were you and Reyes together the entire time, or did he ever leave your sight?"

"We swept the house together," Kelley said. "All by the book."

"When did Reyes start saying he was thirsty?" Mira asked.

"He'd been complaining about that since breakfast at the hotel that morning. He said his coffee tasted burnt, that it had left a bad flavor in his mouth."

"So maybe someone got to him before you even left the hotel that day." Ty scratched his jaw.

Kelley shifted nervously. "There's . . . one more thing."

Ty raised an eyebrow.

Kelley hesitated.

"Well?" said Mira. "Spit it out."

Ty frowned. He tried to cut Mira some slack when it came to her lack of social graces—she'd spent much of her life alone on the streets, after all—but her communications skills left an awful lot to be desired.

"Reyes was an excellent agent," Kelley said, "and I don't want to speak ill of the dead."

"If you have information that might move this case forward," Ty said, "Reyes would want you to share it. He was, as you said, an excellent agent."

Kelley exhaled. "When we were leaving the Johnsons' residence, there was this little ceramic tray by the door with some keys and a bunch of change in it."

Ty nodded.

"Reyes was going on about being thirsty, and he sees these coins, and . . . well . . ."

"He took them," Mira finished.

Kelley looked away. "It was just a couple dollars' worth. Nothing anyone would miss. He said the Johnsons wouldn't mind buying him a drink, seeing as he was working so hard on their behalf."

Mira frowned. "You said there were coins on the floor in the gas station."

"He threw them, I guess. The attendant said Reyes went straight to the fridge and started downing sodas. When he told Reyes he needed to pay first, he reached in his pocket and chucked the coins at the guy. They flew everywhere. His wallet, too. Badge and all. I found it on the floor after . . ." Kelley fell silent.

"Right," Ty said, "we'll take it from here."

Kelley straightened, jaw stiff. "I'd like to help . . . if I can."

Ty pursed his mouth. He could understand Kelley wanting to remain on the case. If Ty hadn't been in a hospital bed himself after Jamal, he would have gone after the fae that dropped a building on them. He nearly had despite the broken leg, until a doctor sedated him. Still, he couldn't have another agent around now that Mira was in town. Too easy to let something slip.

"You're too close to this one," Ty said. "You need to take a step back."

"But—"

"We'll exchange numbers," Ty steamrollered over Kelley's objection. "That way I can keep you apprised of any new developments in the case. And if anything comes up that you can help with, I'll let you know. In the meantime, go get some rest, and try not to dwell on what happened to Reyes or what you could have done differently. Down that road lies madness." He squeezed Kelley's shoulder. "Trust me."

Agent Kelley opened his mouth, closed it, and gave a defeated nod. "If there's anything at all I can do to be useful, please, don't hesitate to call me."

"We'll figure this out," Ty promised. "Whoever did this to Agent Reyes, we'll get them."

"We should start by visiting the gas station," Mira said. "And we should interview the clerk who witnessed the event."

Kelley pulled a small notebook from the inside pocket of his jacket and handed it to Ty. "The address of the gas station, and the name and contact info for the clerk." He glanced at a clock on the wall. "He said he worked ten to six most days, so you'll probably find him at the station."

Ty thanked the coroner for her time, cast one last sympathetic look at Kelley, and led the way out, relieved not to have to spend one more second with Kelley, Reyes, and the ghosts of the dead. Even the stale air in the basement and stairwell seemed fresh compared to the fetid, chemical-laden scents of the morgue. Ty paused on the sidewalk just beyond the glass doors of the lobby and gave himself a shake, willing the afternoon sunshine to chase away the cold that seemed to have seeped into every corner of his being.

"You okay?" Mira rested her fingers lightly against his elbow.

Resisting the urge to cover her hand with his and hold it against his skin, he inhaled, held it, and let the breath out. "Yeah," he said. "Good to go."

She stepped away from him, headed for the driver's side of the truck.

Ty rubbed his arm, chasing away the phantom fingers, and followed, staying well clear of the grate that had ruined his shoe. Once on the road in the relative privacy of the truck, he said, "Thoughts?"

"I'll never look at ham the same way."

"Yeah." He wrinkled his nose. "I could have done without that description." Pushing aside the memory of Mr. Johnson's mutilated corpse, he asked, "Did you notice any rifter taint or residual magic on the bodies?"

Mira shook her head. "But magic doesn't tend to cling to meat very long once it's dead, so that doesn't necessarily rule anything out." She glanced in his direction. "Kelley said they checked for magic in the house. How? I didn't think the PTF employed any magical devices."

Ty chuckled. "Iron dust. Blow it on a person or item possessing fae magic and there should be a reaction, though it's not foolproof."

Mira snorted. "That's barely better than guessing."

He shrugged. "We don't all have a demon on call twenty-four seven, so we make do with what we have. Humans are still way behind the curve in the magic department."

"And whose fault is that?" Mira grumbled.

Ty fell silent. Public perception about magic-users was a touchy subject. Especially in Mira's case. The PTF had only recently started treating human practitioners as more than tools or pets, thanks in large part to a group of paranaturals who'd earned the public's favor by saving the world from a crazed necromancer. Fae still weren't allowed on the force, and rifters, well. . . . There was no scenario in which the upper brass would let a demon into the PTF ranks. Ever. Mira's passenger was as good as a death sentence if the wrong people found out.

"There." Ty pointed out the gas station they were headed to as it came into view on the right, glad for the change in topic.

Chapter 3

Mira

MIRA PULLED AROUND behind the gas station, parking in the shade of a budding maple. She cut the engine and studied the building. "How do you want to play this? Subtle or direct?"

"Direct," Ty said. "This is an official investigation, so there's no need to be sneaky. I'll question the clerk while you scope out the store. Just try not to draw attention to what you're doing."

She shot him a scathing look. "This isn't my first rodeo."

"I know." He exited the truck, and she followed, letting him take the lead.

<He knows "partners" means "equals," right?>

We are equals.

<Then why does he get to decide the approach?>

It's his investigation.

<If we're partners, it's *our* investigation.>

Fine, it's our investigation. But he's got the badge and authority. We'll get to the bottom of this faster if he's the face and we're the support.

<It feel like he's just using us as a magic detector on legs.>

Because that's what's needed right now. You heard him earlier. The best the PTF can do is blow dust in the air and hope it sparks.

<Yeah, that's pretty pathetic, considering they're the people who're supposed to protect the world from magical threats.> The demon shuddered. <How do humans sleep at night?>

In blissful ignorance of the shitstorm raging outside their snow globe existence.

<Or willful denial.>

Or that, she agreed. *Either way, we protect the glass so the rest of the world can sleep.*

<Which is why we should be calling the shots.>

You'd rather talk to the clerk while Ty looks for clues?

<Rift, no! I like his plan. I just think it should have been ours.>

Mira chuckled.

Ty cast her a questioning look over his shoulder.

She shook her head.

A synthesized tone chimed as Ty pushed open the gas station door.

A woman in her mid-forties looked up from sweeping near the back of the store. She wore a pink blouse with an employee name tag pinned over the left breast pocket, tan slacks, and black pumps. Her light-brown hair was twisted into a bun on top of her head.

"Be with you in a moment," she called, and crouched to collect her dustpan. She dumped its contents into a bin near the counter, set the broom in a corner, and beamed at Ty and Mira. "How can I help you?"

Ty flipped open his badge. "I'm Agent Williams with the PTF. I'm investigating an incident that occurred here yesterday."

Her smile melted. "The guy that drank himself to death." She shivered and hugged herself, rubbing her arms. "How awful."

Mira wandered toward the back of the store, where the woman had been sweeping. Five glass doors displayed refrigerated items, but the shelves behind two of the doors were nearly empty. A mere handful of lonely sodas huddled in the bottom corner, overlooked by Reyes's rampage.

"I was told the clerk who witnessed the event would be here today," Ty said. "Can I speak with him?"

"He's *supposed* to be here."

Mira glanced toward the front of the store, surprised by the anger in the woman's voice.

"My name is Maria Sanchez." She set one hand against her chest. Her nails were painted to match her shirt. "I'm the manager here, but I wasn't supposed to be working today. I'm covering until a replacement arrives because Matthew didn't show up for his shift."

Mira turned her gaze back to the empty shelves, but she kept half her attention on Ty's conversation.

Sense anything?

The demon's presence, usually a constant pressure at the back of Mira's mind, swelled. Mira let herself fall back. Her magic was great for blowing shit up, but the demon had other talents. Talents even a skilled practitioner couldn't match. Hazy blue mist overlay Mira's vision. Ty and the station manager became person-shaped smudges made of shifting smoke.

<There's nothing here.>

Mira sagged, unsurprised but disappointed. *Whatever magic drove Reyes to drink must have dissipated already. I doubt we'll find anything at the Johnsons' house either.*

<I'm going to try something.>

Mira glanced over her shoulder. The manager was waving her arms, complaining to Ty about the mess Reyes had made, the loss of inventory, as if a dip in profits were the true tragedy rather than the loss of a man's life. *Will this draw attention?*

<I don't know.>

What are you going to do?

<Look into the past.>

Mira's thoughts ground to a halt as she tried to wrap her brain around the demon's casual reference to the near impossible. Time manipulation was sovereign-level magic.

Do you really think you can do that?

<I'm not sure. That's why I said *try*.>

Mira thought about arguing. A year ago, Mira's demon wouldn't have had the juice to even attempt magic on this scale, but they'd grown stronger recently. Even Mira wasn't sure what they were capable of these days. Biting her tongue, she settled back, anxious and alert. *Have faith*, she told herself. If she'd had control over her body at that moment, she would have touched the St. Michael pendant around her neck. Instead she simply said a silent prayer that the demon knew what they were doing.

A smoky doppelganger of Mira laced with colored streaks of detail backtracked to the counter, then out of the station with a hazy version of Ty. The manager's past self came toward Mira and started sweeping. Other shapes came and went, moving faster as time rewound. The Rift connected all things, and everything left an imprint. The Rift remembered.

Mira gasped, but the sound never left her lips. She was just a voice at the back of her head right now. *I can't believe you're doing this!*

<I got the idea from that time warp we did in Baltimore.> Strain laced the demon's voice.

A pounding ache built behind Mira's eyes. The people shapes grew less dense, blurring and overlapping. A flicker of red flashed in vibrant contrast to the swirling blue mist.

What was that?

The demon smirked in satisfaction. <Magic.>

Mira's knees buckled. She grabbed a shelf to steady herself but only succeeded in toppling a display of powdered donuts. She hit the floor. Packages scattered around her.

"Mira!" Ty was at her side, supporting her shoulders as she sat up.

Dizzying sparks of light danced in her vision, but the blue mist was gone. The demon had withdrawn to the deepest recess of her mind, exhausted. Mira wasn't faring much better. That spell had taken a lot of juice, and Mira's body was the battery.

The synthetic doorbell *bing-bong*ed. A tall woman with blue hair and plump cheeks looked around frantically as she stepped into the station. Her gaze latched onto the manager, and she hurried forward. "I just saw Matthew being loaded into the back of an ambulance!" She was out of breath, as though she'd been running. "His hands were all bloody, and he was screaming about gold. The whole place was crawling with cops."

Ty lifted Mira to her feet and steadied her. She waved him off. "I'm fine." Focusing on the newcomer, she asked, "Where did you see this?"

The woman looked from Mira and Ty to the station manager, who said, "They're PTF. Answer them."

The woman licked her lips and hoisted a large, purple purse higher on her shoulder. "It was at the construction site I walk past on my way here. Two blocks north, then hang a right. You can't miss it."

Ty caught Mira's gaze and asked, "You okay to run?"

She narrowed her eyes. "Try to keep up."

She was out the door three steps ahead of Ty, who shouted a hurried, "Thank you," over his shoulder as he pelted out of the station. As soon as she cleared the building, she caught the sound of sirens in the distance. She turned north. Despite her confident words to Ty, Mira's legs dragged like weights as she ran. Ty caught up in the first block, then matched her pace. The demon had used a lot of energy, and Mira's body was paying the price. She glanced at the backs of her hands. Her cracked cuticles bore a slightly purple tint.

¡Coño! When the demon used power, that energy came out of Mira's hide, literally. Use too much and the damage began to show. Most demons didn't care about the damage they inflicted on their hosts, using them up until they were destroyed—the fate of every rifter Mira had ever come across, save herself and one other. Mira and her demon had found a way around that by siphoning energy from other rifters, but the balance they maintained was delicate, and time manipulation was no small trick.

Surely Ty would have mentioned if I'd developed noticeable cracks on my face . . . But she couldn't shake the worry that her possession was starting to show. Not when they were running toward a scene full of police officers. Gritting her teeth, she asked Ty, "Am I showing any puppet lines?"

Ty craned his neck to examine her face as they ran. "You're pale, but still human-looking. What did you do back there?"

"I'll tell you later, but there was definitely magic involved in Reyes's death."

"Rifter magic? Fae? Practitioner?"

Mira prodded the demon sleeping in her subconscious but got no response. "Not sure yet."

They rounded the right corner two blocks from the gas station and came to an abrupt halt. Three police cruisers circled the entrance to a construction site, and a crowd of pedestrians blocked half the street. While all the official vehicles had their lights flashing an epilepsy-inducing strobe of red and blue, the siren Mira heard from the gas station was steadily fading into the distance.

Ty pulled out his badge as the two of them approached the police line. Waving down the nearest officer, he said, "What's the situation here?"

The young man in uniform took one look at Ty's badge, blanched, and said, "We responded to a 911 call placed by the construction foreman. When his crew came back from lunch, there was a man digging a hole in the foundation *with his bare hands*. The workers tried to pull him away, but he got violent. So they left him to dig and called us. By the time we arrived, his hands were—" The officer pressed a fist to his mouth and shook his head.

"Do you know the man's name?"

"The ID in his wallet was for Matthew Clark. He lives just around the corner."

"And works at the gas station two blocks south of here," Ty said. "I need to interview him. Where was he taken?"

"The ambulance is on its way to St. Vincent. I just hope he doesn't come to before they get there." He shook his head. His gaze grew distant. "That guy had to be jacked up on something. It took four officers to wrestle him down so the EMTs could sedate him."

Mira waved a hand to get the man's attention. "Can you show us this hole he was digging?"

The officer led them past the construction fence, which doubled as paid advertising space. They walked past banners for Wendy's newest chicken burger, a spring sale at Duluth Trading Co., and an upcoming exhibit at the Baker Heritage Museum about miners finding gold in the Pacific Northwest. Mira nudged Ty and nodded toward the museum sign.

Ty cleared his throat and asked, "Did Mr. Clark say anything?"

"Nothing that made sense," the officer said. "He kept yelling that he had to get the gold. We told him there was no gold here, but he just kept saying he needed it. He needed the gold."

A group of construction workers stood off to one side of the area, near stacks of rebar, steel I-beams, two-by-fours, and sheets of plywood.

Two officers seemed to be taking their statements. The cordoned-off zone was hard-packed earth around a concrete foundation that would someday become a new business complex. A light breeze ruffled the advertisements and brought Mira the scent of blood.

Time to wake up, buddy. She gave the groggy demon a mental shove. *We need to check out this site.*

The demon stirred sluggishly. <That was a bad idea.>

You verified the presence of magic at the time of Agent Reyes's death.

<Fat whoop. If I drive much more today, I'm gonna start bleeding through.>

This is a fresh site. If there's magic to be found here, we can't miss the opportunity to identify it. We still don't know what kind of paranatural we're hunting. Heck, they may still be in the area.

<Fine. But don't come crying to me when I ruin your complexion.>

Just . . . don't go overboard. Okay?

<Do the thing. Don't do the thing.> The demon gave Mira a mental eye roll. <Make up your mind.>

No more big spells. Just look for any nearby sources of magic.

"You good?" Ty's question, and his hand on her arm, startled Mira out of her mental conversation.

"Yeah, just . . . thinking."

"Mm hmm." He gestured to a hole near the edge of the poured foundation. "What do you think about this?"

Mira glanced around and saw the officer who'd led them to the hole walking back toward the perimeter. Ty must have shooed him away while she was distracted. *Smart.*

<It's nice to have someone who can take care of the mundane stuff while we focus on what's important,> said the demon.

A smile tugged at Mira's lips. She crouched next to the hole and leaned over to get a better look. Matthew had dug about four feet deep of dirt, rock, and clay in a three-foot diameter. And if the construction workers' story was true, he'd done it in less than a lunch break. Bloody smears streaked the edges and bottom of the hole along finger-width grooves. Mira hated to imagine what Matthew's hands must look like.

Taking a deep breath, she settled on her knees and let the demon take over.

Remember, just a quick look.

<Yeah, yeah.>

The haze of the Rift pressed into Mira's vision. She looked in the hole, then around the construction site. No flashes of color, and no magical beings shining like beacons in the Rift. The demon settled back. Mira blinked.

"Well?" asked Ty.

"Nothing," she said. "If there was magic here, it's already gone."

"Damn it." He ran one hand over his close-cropped hair and braced the other against his hip. "Let's get to the hospital and see what we can get out of Matthew Clark."

Chapter 4

Mira

MIRA CRANED HER neck to see St. Vincent Hospital through the windshield; it was a multistory, beige building, wider than it was tall. She rested her cheek against her hands where they draped the top of the steering wheel and exhaled, resisting the urge to close her eyes. *That stunt at the gas station took a lot out of us. If Matthew Clark turns out to be a rifter, are you gonna be good for a fight?*

<If you can fight, I can fight.>

"Do you need to sit this one out?"

Mira blinked and straightened, trying to clear the tired fog clinging to her thoughts. She gave Ty what she hoped was a reassuring smile. "We're okay."

"Really? 'Cause you look hungover."

She rubbed her temples. "Just a little magic-burned."

"And it's starting to look like you're wearing eyeliner."

Mira glanced in her side mirror. Dark shadows ringed her eyes, but the skin hadn't started to crack yet. She clenched her jaw. She hated to admit weakness, but she'd hate getting IDed as a rifter even more. Grudgingly, she said, "I may need a little pick-me-up."

Ty offered his hand, palm up. "Not too much. I need to be coherent."

The demon stirred. <Lips work better.>

Leave it, Mira warned. She clasped Ty's hand, as if she were going to shake it, and let the demon rise once more to the surface. Ribbons of energy, invisible to the naked eye, flowed from Ty into Mira. She couldn't see them like she could see the demons she pulled from rifter bodies with this same technique, but the gossamer threads tickled as they brushed her fingers and sank into her skin. Her lethargy faded.

Ty's grip remained warm and firm. It had taken some time for him to come to grips with the fact that Mira and her demon survived by draining energy from other living beings, and longer still for him to trust her enough to volunteer. Not that she could blame him. Most of her donors ended up as desiccated husks. That's why she fed almost exclusively from rifters these days. But every now and then she needed a snack between meals. Luckily, she'd had years to work on her control. A sip or two wouldn't hurt anyone. At least not permanently. Though she still felt like a monster when she fed off regular humans.

That's enough. Mira forced her way to the surface, trading places with the demon, who sank into the background with a satisfied purr.

Ty yawned and rubbed his eyes.

Mira released him, letting her fingertips rest for a moment against his before breaking the contact. "How do you feel?" she asked.

"A little tired." He met her gaze and smile. "Nothing a quick nap won't fix." He reached toward her face.

Mira shrank back. They both froze.

Ty lowered his hand. "Your puppet lines are gone."

"Oh," she said. "Good."

The demon chuckled.

Mira blushed.

"Let's get inside." Turning away, Ty let himself out of the truck.

<Skittish much?>

Mira stepped out of the truck and slammed the door.

"Damn it!" Ty shouted.

Mira hurried around the hood, tensed for a fight.

Ty balanced on one foot on the hospital sidewalk. He kicked his other foot, the one with the torn shoe. Water dripped off it, scattering ripples in the puddle beside him.

Mira relaxed, then grinned. "You should be more careful where you step."

He glared at her. "How was I supposed to know there was a freaking pothole in the gutter right there?"

Hopping over the deceptively deep puddle, Mira grabbed Ty's elbow and steered him toward the hospital entrance.

"It soaked through my sock because of that damn hole from earlier," he muttered, squelching with every other step.

Mira suppressed a laugh. *Ty's always so fastidious about his appearance,* she thought, pleased at the chance to use one of her "words of the day." *It's good for him to get a little dirty now and then.*

<Yeah, maybe he'll loosen up and do something crazy, like pack his toothbrush in a different pocket.>

That pushed Mira over the edge; she couldn't help but laugh.

The nurse at the reception desk took one look at Ty's badge, coupled with his scowl, and directed them to room 309, where Matthew Clark was being prepped for surgery.

The smell of antiseptic and the quiet hum of lifesaving devices filled the halls. Matthew's room boasted a private bed and a window overlooking a courtyard on the back side of the building. That was where the comfort ended. Matthew Clark was handcuffed to metal rails on either side of his bed. His hands were heavily bandaged, and blood stained the thickly wrapped gauze. Matthew's head lolled from side to side. His eyelids fluttered, never quite opening. His lips quivered, as if he were trying to speak but couldn't force his mouth into the right shape. Three people stood around his bed, all in scrubs and white coats. One injected something into a tube attached to Matthew's arm. Another wrote something on a clipboard, while the last used a thumb to lift Matthew's eyelid and flicked a penlight back and forth across his vision.

What do you think? Mira kept her lips pressed tight to avoid accidentally speaking out loud.

<Not a rifter,> the demon said, <but there's definitely *some* kind of magic clinging to him.>

You can't identify it?

<Like you could do any better.>

"He's coming out too fast," said the man with the penlight. "We'll need to up the dosage."

The woman holding the clipboard grunted. "I want him in surgery as soon as possible. There's still a chance we can save his fingers."

Ty cleared his throat.

The woman with the clipboard glanced over. "Are you next of kin?"

Ty and Mira both shook their heads, then Ty pulled out his badge. "PTF. We need to question Mr. Clark."

"You can have him after surgery." She set down Matthew's file. "Until then, he's staying under."

"Assuming I can find the right dosage," muttered the man who'd put away his flashlight and was staring at his patient with a frown.

The remaining woman said, "You're the best anesthesiologist in the city. You'll figure it out." She set her now-empty syringe on a metal tray next to a bottle and carried the set out of the room, squeezing past Ty and Mira near the door.

The man shook his head. Looking at his colleague, he said, "We may have to induce a coma to keep him fully under." Then he followed the nurse out, completely ignoring Ty and Mira.

"What's his prognosis?" Ty asked the remaining doctor.

"Despite losing a lot of blood, his chances of survival are pretty high. Whether or not he'll be able to use his hands again . . ." She shrugged. "I need to get him into surgery as soon as possible, but his metabolism is through the roof. We're having trouble keeping him sedated. And when he gains even the slightest bit of awareness, he becomes violent." She gestured to the handcuffs. "Hence the restraints. He's already injured two EMTs and an ER nurse. Since he's proven dangerous to both the staff and himself, we can't risk starting the surgery if there's any chance he'll wake up."

<We could take care of that,> suggested the demon. <And I could use another snack. That sip we took off Ty was barely an appetizer.>

Not with a witness. Mira chewed her lower lip, but before she could come up with a reason to clear the room, the door burst open behind her. A stocky man with a reddish beard and startled green eyes stumbled through the door, colliding with Mira. She pivoted and let the man's momentum carry him to the floor. He scrambled up without missing a beat, completely ignoring the three people staring at him, and, grabbing the bed rail for support, sobbed Matthew's name.

<That was quite the entrance.> The demon's voice rang with amusement. <Do you think he's a comedian?>

He's upset, Mira replied.

<That doesn't mean he's not a clown.>

"Next of kin, I presume?" asked the doctor.

"I'm his fiancé." The man snuffled and wiped his nose. Tears streaked his cheeks, filtering into his beard. "What happened? Will he be okay?"

The doctor glanced at Ty and Mira, then at Matthew in the bed.

Ty stepped forward, showed the newcomer his badge, and asked, "Has your fiancé shown any odd behavior lately? Changes in his personality?"

The man sniffed again and shook his head. "He's been stressed since . . . There was this guy that died at the gas station where Matty works. But who wouldn't be stressed out by that? I mean, the guy died literally *right in front of him*." He gestured with his hands, as though he were holding the scene for them to inspect.

"That's all?" Mira asked. "Just stress about the dead guy?"

He glared at her. "Isn't that enough?"

The doctor cleared her throat. "I understand that this is a difficult situation for you Mr. . . .?"

"Berkeley. Calvin Berkeley."

". . . Mr. Berkeley, but do you have contact information for Mr. Clark's next of kin? There are some decisions that need to be made regarding his treatment."

"I'm his emergency contact," shouted Mr. Berkeley. "You can discuss them with me!"

The doctor frowned. "A fiancé is not a spouse, Mr. Berkeley. I'm afraid you don't have the legal authority to—"

"Dammit, Matthew! I told you! How many times did I say that I didn't care?" The distraught fiancé turned to shout at his unconscious partner. "But no. You just had to have gold!"

Mira raised her eyebrows.

"Wait," Ty said, stepping forward to grab Mr. Berkeley's arm. "What about gold?"

"The rings." Berkeley shook Ty off. "We'd have been married a year ago if Matty hadn't insisted on gold rings. But it takes forever to save up enough to afford them on a station attendant's and social worker's salaries. We've already postponed the wedding three times." He turned his anger back on the man in the bed. "Just look where that's got us. The doctor won't even talk to me." His expression softened. He reached out and gently caressed Matthew's cheek. "But that's my Matty. Go big or go home."

The doctor patted Mr. Berkeley on the back and said, "Let's take a walk to my office. I'll tell you what I can about Mr. Clark's condition, and maybe you can help me get in touch with the rest of his family."

Mr. Berkeley nodded. All the fight seemed to have drained out of him when he touched Matthew's face. He allowed the doctor to steer him toward the door, one arm around his shoulders. His feet dragged over the polished tiles.

The doctor cast a glance over Mr. Berkeley's back at Mira and Ty. "Mr. Clark won't be talking any time soon. I trust you two can see yourselves out."

Ty nodded, but as soon as the door swung closed, he spun on Mira. "Well? Anything?"

"He's not a rifter," she said, gesturing to his bandaged hands, "obviously. But he does have magic on him. Someone else's magic."

"Rift magic?"

<More likely fae magic,> said the demon. <Judging by the feel.>

Mira sighed. She hated dealing with the fae. Not that demons and rifters were any easier, but at least she got a good meal at the end. Fae were . . . incompatible. "Number Two says we're probably looking for a fae."

<Number Two? What am I, a turd?>

Well, I can hardly say 'the demon says' in a public place, now can I? Mira countered.

<Yeah, but Number Two? That's the best you can come up with?>

If you want a better name, how about finally picking one for yourself? I'm getting tired of not having anything to call you.

<I've told you before, that's not gonna happen. Demons don't do names.>

Then suck it up, Number Two.

Ty chuckled.

Mira glared at him, suddenly unsure if she'd said any of that conversation out loud. "What are you smiling about?"

His grin widened. "I'm just imagining what 'Number Two'"—he made finger quotes—"had to say about that nickname to get you to make that face."

Mira rolled her eyes. "Are we in kindergarten? Can we just focus, please?"

"Fine." Ty raised his hands in surrender. "Fae. So maybe a compulsion spell?"

"Maybe. Let me take a closer look now that the peanut gallery is gone." She shot Ty a scathing look. "Mostly."

He laughed. Circling the bed, he picked up a plastic bag full of fabric. "I'll look through his belongings, see if there's anything to connect him to this case besides seeing Reyes die."

His smile evaporated as though it had never existed, as if his face had never known the shape of a smile.

Mira turned awkwardly away, unsure how best to deal with Ty's fluctuating emotions, and set her hand against Matthew's forehead, cringing at the sweat that transferred to her palm. *Can you confirm the magic is fae?*

The demon rose to the surface just enough to affect the physical world. The blue haze of the Rift drifted over Mira's vision. Energy flowed through Mira's palm, tingling like pins and needles against her skin. She reached with that energy toward the rosy glow lodged in Matthew's brain. A wave of nausea rolled over her. Her legs turned to noodles. She grabbed the bed rail for support.

<Yep,> the demon said, <definitely fae. And don't ask me to remove it. We are NOT doing that again.>

Mira clung to the rail, trying not to vomit. *Can you tell how it's affecting him?*

<Since the magic is centered in his brain, it's probably some kind of subconscious compulsion spell.>

Can you drain his energy without absorbing any of the magic?

Mira sensed the mental equivalent of the demon cracking their knuckles. <Just watch me.>

Only enough to keep him sleepy, Mira warned. *We don't want him dying on the operating table.* She resisted the urge to glance at Ty. One of the rules he'd insisted on when their partnership began was that she never drain energy from an innocent without their consent. She'd mostly succeeded, but sometimes good intentions had to bow in the face of circumstantial necessity. In this case, she figured Ty would understand. She was draining Matthew for his own sake as much as hers. The guy needed to be calm enough for surgery, and the magic in his brain was like an adrenaline bomb forcing him to act. But even if Ty agreed with the practicality of draining Matthew, the process would make him uncomfortable. It always did. Feeding from a semiconscious human, no matter the circumstance, already made Mira feel like a freak. She didn't relish the added judgment of an audience.

<I won't tell him if you don't.>

The flow of energy between Mira and Matthew switched direction. Mira's knees no longer felt weak. Her stomach settled. Matthew stopped twitching, finally resting easy against his pillow. His breathing evened out.

Mira lifted her hand, breaking the connection. *Good job.* Smiling from the giddy feeling feeding always gave her, she turned toward Ty to confirm their suspicions about the spell. He held Matthew's jeans in one hand. His other came out of one of the pockets enveloped in a cherry glow, as if he clutched a red star in his hand.

Mira reached out and shouted, "Don't touch that!"

Ty jerked as though burned. Whatever he'd been holding fell to the floor, but Mira's warning had come too late. A wisp of dull red snaked through the smoky energy swirling through Ty, settling like a cancer in his head.

Can you—

<No.>

I didn't even—

<I know what you're going to ask. The answer is no.> The demon's voice lacked its usual playfulness as they vacated the driver's seat, leaving Mira in full control of her body once more. <Sorry.>

Mira joined Ty to look at the clustered items he'd removed from Matthew's pocket. The mist of the Rift faded with the demon's withdrawal, and the hospital room resolved into harsh detail. The glaring beacon Mira had failed to see in time dimmed and winked out, leaving a dull and dented quarter. Without the demon's vision, the quarter looked no different from the ordinary nickels and dimes that accompanied it. It was just a coin. Simple. Innocuous. Easy to pass around. She shuddered.

"What's the matter?" Anxiety flitted beneath the surface of Ty's calm exterior. "Why did you shout?"

Mira pointed at the quarter. "That coin is enchanted with fae magic. I'm guessing Matthew picked it up after Agent Reyes threw it at him."

Ty blanched. "And Reyes got it from the tray at the Johnsons' house."

Mira nodded. "We were never looking for a person. These victims are being killed by a cursed object." She took a shaky breath. "And you're next."

Chapter 5

Ty

"BUT WE CAN break it, right?" Ty forced himself to smile. "Melt it down. Coat it in iron. The PTF has destroyed artifacts before."

"The PTF has *neutralized* artifacts before," Mira corrected. "I doubt you've ever truly destroyed one."

"Same difference."

She shook her head. "Not even remotely. Locking the coin in an iron box might prevent the curse from spreading, but that won't help those who're already infected, including you and Matthew."

Panic prickled at the back of Ty's neck as his confidence wavered. "I barely touched it. Maybe I'm not—"

"You are."

He pressed his lips together and focused on his breathing, giving her assertion a moment to sink in. He didn't *feel* enchanted, but he trusted Mira. And Reyes hadn't seen anything wrong with guzzling drain cleaner at the gas station, so clearly Ty couldn't rely on his instincts in this situation. "Okay," he said. "So how do we break the curse?"

"I'm no expert, but as I understand it there are two ways to break an enchantment. Overwhelm it with a massive amount of magic, or bargain with the person who cast the spell in the first place. The first usually results in a massive magical explosion."

"So we *are* looking for a person."

"Specifically, we're looking for the fae who owns this coin." She pointed again at the unassuming quarter.

Ty looked down, but his attention wandered to the hole in his shoe. He wiggled his cold toes, hating the feel of soggy sock pressed against his skin. *Maybe I should have taken the time to get a new pair right away. Then the puddle wouldn't have been a problem. And how's anyone supposed to take me seriously when I have a hole in my shoe? It's unprofessional.*

"Hey." Mira waved a hand in front of his face. "It's gonna be okay. We'll figure this out."

Ty blinked, pushing aside the spiraling tangent his mind had taken.

"Yeah," he said. "Of course." He cleared his throat. "First things first. We need to make sure no one else touches this coin." Using a paper cup on a tray beside Matthew's bed, he pushed the coin into an evidence bag.

"It probably can't curse you twice," Mira said.

He glanced at her. She scratched an itch on the back of one leg with her sneaker.

Those look comfortable, he thought. *Not that I'd wear sneakers on a case. They'd give the wrong impression.* He shook his head, clearing the thought. "Better safe than sorry. Maybe prolonged exposure speeds up the process or something."

Mira frowned. "Could be. The spell seems to have affected Agent Reyes faster than it did Matthew, so there's probably some variable we're unaware of. Although I seriously doubt a thin layer of plastic will offer any protection."

Ty stood, lifting the evidence bag with the cursed coin by the very corner. "I don't really want to carry this around with me, but . . ."

"Yeah. Not a lot of options here." Mira sounded apologetic, as though she'd somehow let him down by being unable to carry the coin herself.

With a sigh and a grimace, Ty gingerly slid the coin into his pants pocket. He shifted his weight, imagining he could feel the coin burning like a flame against his thigh. *It's just my imagination. I didn't notice anything the first time I touched it.*

Taking a deep breath to clear his head, he said, "Let's go over what we know. People have only been dying from this thing for about a week, so whoever cast the spell had to be in the area recently."

"And depending on why they cast the spell, they might have stuck around to see the results."

He snapped his fingers. "Good point. Killers like to see their handiwork. So if we trace the coin's path back to the first death and figure out who wanted to kill them, maybe we find whoever enchanted the coin."

Mira nodded. "Matthew was the last person to touch the coin before you. He picked it up at the gas station after Reyes threw it on the floor."

"We think," Ty interjected—always a stickler for precision, even in the face of speculation. "And Reyes took the coin out of a tray at the Johnson crime scene. Since Mrs. Johnson was the one acting crazy, let's assume the husband didn't touch the coin."

"Speaking of which, are you feeling anything?" Mira asked. "Any sudden urges to eat people or jump out a window?"

Ty shook his head. "Other than being freaked out that I'm cursed and pissed that my shoe got ruined . . . nope. No suicidal impulses."

"That's something, at least," she said. "Hopefully we have a little time."

Ty gestured to Matthew, now sleeping soundly in the hospital bed. "He was fine for more than a day before he started digging that hole."

"But Reyes didn't last two hours," Mira countered.

He glared. "Thanks."

"Sorry," she mumbled. "Just being practical. We don't know how long you've got, so we need to hurry."

"Right." Ty swept a hand over his buzzed hair. "Mrs. Johnson went to a yoga parlor, a grocery store, and a bank on the day she died, but I guess she could have gotten the coin the day before."

"Didn't you say another person who died recently worked at a grocery store?"

Ty perked up. "Good point. If Mrs. Johnson paid for her groceries in cash, she might have gotten the coin as change. In which case, the cashier who died probably had the coin in her drawer."

"What grocery store did she work at?" Mira asked.

"Let's give Agent Kelley a call. He can pull the address."

"And while we're at it, let's ask for a list of *all* the recent deaths in the area," she said. "Maybe not everyone died in a weird enough way to get noticed."

Nodding, Ty shoved Matthew's jeans and shirt back into the "personal belongings" bag. He hesitated to pick up the remaining coins on the floor, but forced himself to collect them and dropped them in the bag as well. He set the bag on top of Matthew's shoes, a pair of blue fabric espadrilles. He lifted one of the shoes and shook his head at the mud caked in the soft tread. *Disgraceful. I wouldn't be caught dead in these.*

"You coming?" Mira called from the door.

Ty set the shoe down and followed her out.

"THE GROCERY STORE cashier worked and died at Tenth and Columbia," Agent Kelley said through the phone.

Ty relayed the address to Mira, then turned his attention back to the call. "I'd also like you to pull up any and all deaths reported in the Portland area in the past . . . let's say three weeks."

"You got it. I'll start pulling files."

"I'll text you my email. Send them over as soon as you can."

Ty started to lower the phone, but Kelley said, "Thanks for not benching me. I really . . . I need to be a part of this one."

"Yeah," Ty said. "I get it." He disconnected the call and exhaled. He glanced at Mira. "If I'm . . . out of commission—"

Mira shook her head. "It won't come to that."

"—I want you to finish this case and send your findings to Agent Kelley. He'll take care of the rest." Ty licked his lips. "Make sure no one touches the coin. The PTF has a vault for artifacts like this. They can bury it."

"We don't know for sure physical contact is the only trigger," Mira pointed out.

"We could fill a whole damn vault with what we don't know about this thing." He rubbed his eyes. "Where's a fae when you need one?"

Mira snorted. "Maybe if the PTF loosened the reins on who's allowed to serve and protect—"

He raised a hand to ward her off. "You know I agree with you, but we have to work with what we have right now."

Mira pulled into the grocery store parking lot and cut the engine. "We're barely a block from the Johnsons' neighborhood. This has to be where the wife bought her groceries." She twisted on the seat and gave Ty an appraising look. "I'm not going to have to tackle you in the liquor aisle, am I?"

"I *could* use a drink." He forced a smile. "But no; no cravings at the moment."

They made their way inside. Clouds had rolled in, turning the sky to a flat gray that hid the sun. Even the trees and buildings seemed colorless under that sky. Metal carts with squeaky wheels rattled across the pavement as shoppers pushed their purchases to their cars. Children called for their parents' attention in checkout lines, pointing to gum, balloons, stuffed animals, or whatever impulse buy caught their attention.

Ty flashed his badge at the first worker to cross his path and asked to see the manager.

"What's this about?" asked a small woman with dark skin and darker hair woven into dozens of braids. She wore business-casual clothes and practical black pumps.

"We're looking into the death of one of your employees," Ty said, lifting his gaze back to the woman's face. "Claire Dawson."

"Oh." The manager shuffled her feet. "There's no mystery or anything. She was hit by a bus."

"After raiding the cash from her till and running out of the building yelling about freedom," Mira said. "Does that seem like normal behavior to you?"

"Of course not! I just . . . What did you want to ask?" The woman's eyes darted side to side, as if assessing how much impact this conversation might have on the nearby shoppers, should they overhear.

"Just a couple questions," Ty assured her, "then we'll be out of your hair. Did Claire exhibit any strange behavior in the days leading up to her death?"

"Other than those last moments, no."

"What can you tell us about her as a person?"

"She was a good worker. Showed up on time. Always willing to take extra shifts and work holidays." The manager shrugged. "We have a lot of turnover here. I don't get to know most of the employees very well. If you want to know more about Claire, I suggest you talk to Amy Yang." She pointed to the checker in lane four, a slender woman with straight black hair held in a butterfly clip. She wore a beige shirt tucked into black slacks. "Those two seemed pretty close."

"Then by all means," Ty said, "please introduce us."

The manager approached lane four, Ty and Mira in tow, and waited for the current customer to complete their transaction. Up close, the cashier was even thinner looking, with narrow lips and sunken eyes lined with heavy makeup. "Amy, these people need to talk to you about Claire. Why don't you step outside? I'll cover your register."

The cashier's eyes widened. She looked from the manager to Ty and Mira, back to the manager, then nodded and left her check-out stand without a word. Ty and Mira followed her out the main entrance and around a corner, where a small, round picnic table was chained to the trunk of a tree. Her scuffed white sneakers drew Ty's attention as she sat on the table and tucked one leg under her. Her other foot rested on the bench seat.

"What do you want to know about Claire?" Amy had a high, nasal voice.

"What can you tell us?" Mira countered.

Amy shrugged. "She was a single mom raising two boys, nine and thirteen. Her loser ex was a drunk who never paid child support, so she worked her ass off to make ends meet. Took every shit shift the manager threw her way."

"Do you think that's why she took the money out of her register?" Ty asked. "For her kids?"

"Those tills hold maybe a few hundred bucks at any given time. What kind of moron would risk prison for that?" Amy shook her head. She pulled a pack of cigarettes out of her back pocket, slipped one into her mouth, and lit it. She took a deep breath and exhaled a cloud of smoke. "Claire wasn't a moron. She loved those boys. She never would have done anything that might risk leaving them alone." She shook her head again and took another pull. "It makes no sense."

Ty coughed and waved a hand to clear the smoke. "Would you mind putting that out?"

Amy frowned, looked at the cigarette in her hand as though noticing it for the first time, and stubbed it in an ashtray already overflowing with half-burnt butts. "Sorry. Nervous habit. I know I should quit."

"Then why don't you?" Mira asked, blunt as ever.

Ty rolled his eyes.

"It's not easy to shake an addiction," Amy said. "Even one you know might kill you."

"Were there any regular customers who came in the day or two before Claire died that haven't been around since?" Ty asked, steering the conversation in a more useful direction.

Amy shrugged. "Some people come in every day. Some come once a month. I don't really keep track." She snapped her fingers. "That cannibal lady I saw on the news was in the store the day Claire died. Could that be important?"

Ty nodded. "It certainly could be. No other people exhibiting odd behavior that you know of?"

"We called the cops on this one guy a few days ago for peeing on a display, but other than that—" She shook her head. "I wish I could be of more help, but I really don't know why Claire did what she did. I should probably get back to work."

"Just one more question," Ty said.

Amy looked at him expectantly.

"Do you sell shoes at this store?"

Mira frowned.

Amy blinked, as if trying to decide if he was joking. "Um, no, but there's a DSW just up the road."

"Thanks for your time," Mira said. "You can go now."

"We're sorry for your loss," Ty called at the departing woman's back.

Mira slapped his arm hard enough to sting. "Seriously? You're that worried about the hole in your shoe?"

"Sorry, I just thought . . ." Ty shook his head, unsure *what* he'd been thinking. It wasn't like him to lose focus during an interview. "Forget it. Won't happen again."

Mira gave him a worried look. "Just how much are you thinking about your shoes right now?"

"I'm not about to start eating them, if that's what you're asking."

"Good," she said. "Make sure it stays that way. We still don't know what triggered the victims' obsessions." Mira dug her fingers along her scalp, fluffing her hair. A few strands of the white stripe on the left fell in front of her golden eye. "This is a dead end. Even if Claire died because she handled the coin, hundreds of people shop here every day. That coin could have come from anywhere."

"We found out Claire was strapped for cash," Ty said, trying to put a positive spin on the situation. "Then she grabbed whatever cash was nearest and made a break for it."

"Right into traffic," Mira said flatly.

"Yeah, well, I think we can all agree that none of these people were thinking clearly once the curse took hold."

She gave him a pointed look, which he waved away.

"I'm fine. Anyway, Claire needed money, so she took it even though it was a terrible idea. Reyes was thirsty when he picked up the coin, and he ended up drinking himself to death. Matthew wanted gold for his wedding rings . . ." He gestured for her to finish the sentence.

"So he started digging next to a sign advertising a mining exhibit about gold found in the Pacific Northwest," Mira said. "Okay, I see where you're going with this. Mrs. Johnson was cooking pot roast, so . . . she was hungry, I guess?"

"Specifically for meat. She ate the ground beef, too, before she started on her husband."

"So whatever a person is craving at the moment they touch the coin, that's what they become obsessed with?" Mira shook her head. "But Mrs. Johnson didn't start cooking the pot roast until *after* she got the coin."

"She was buying the ingredients for it when she got her change, though, so it was already on her mind."

"Okay." Mira crossed her arms. "I'm assuming, when you touched the coin, you were thinking about . . ."

They both looked down.

"The hole in my shoe," Ty confirmed.

Chapter 6

Mira

<SO TY'S GOING to obsesses about his appearance?> The demon gave the mental equivalent of a shrug. <That's nothing new.>

This goes way beyond Ty's usual fastidiousness. Mira glared at the tiny patch of white sock peeking through the hole in the side of Ty's shoe. She bit her lip, recalling the way she'd laughed when he stepped in the puddle. Now, that stupid soggy sock and torn leather might be the death of him . . . though she couldn't imagine how.

"Maybe we should make a quick trip to that DSW Amy mentioned," Ty said. "The answer might be to just give the curse what it wants."

"Like Reyes tried to quench his thirst?" Mira shook her head. The sick, squirming feeling in her gut grew stronger as she imagined Ty losing control. "The coin's an inanimate object. You can't reason with it or buy it off. You break the curse, or you die."

Ty scowled at her. "You're making it very difficult for me to stay positive right now."

"The priority is to keep you alive, and denial's not going to help with that."

Ty opened his mouth, but his phone chimed, cutting him off. He glanced at the screen, poked it, and said, "Kelley just forwarded the police files on all the recent deaths in the area."

Mira took a deep breath, glad of any distraction that would prevent her from examining the fear she was experiencing too closely. Especially if said distraction gave them an actionable lead to follow. She pressed against Ty's shoulder so she could see the screen. "Anything jump out?"

Ty hesitated long enough that she looked up. He was staring not at the phone, but at her. He cleared his throat, shifted his gaze back to the phone, and scrolled through the list.

<Too bad he wasn't looking at you like that when he touched the coin. Maybe you both could have gotten over this whole "no sex with my partner" thing.>

Mira swallowed and fought to control the heat climbing her neck. *Ha ha. I'm sure you'd love that . . . until he had a heart attack or died of dehydration or something. Besides, who's to say thinking about sex would have led to sex with me? Maybe he'd be going after every piece of ass in the city.*

<As opposed to shoes.> The demon snorted.

It's not funny.

<Are you kidding? It's freaking hilarious. How does a person even die from a shoe obsession?>

That drained the blush off Mira's face. *Let's not find out.*

". . . the most suspicious. What do you think?" Ty's voice broke into her thoughts.

"Hm? About what?" Mira looked at the phone, then up at him. He smelled like cloves and whiskey.

Ty scowled. "Were you even listening?"

<Busted.>

She shook her head. "Nope."

He stared at her for a good three seconds, then rolled his eyes and said, "Aside from the victims we already know are connected to the coin, there've been two shootings, one heroin overdose, and a plane crash."

"Plane crash? Those are pretty rare."

"Especially considering that the plane crashed because the pilot jumped out mid-flight."

"What? Why wasn't that on your earlier list of weird deaths?"

"I didn't know about the pilot until Kelley sent me this file. The article I read online reported the cause of the crash as mechanical failure. Now the police are thinking drugs may have been involved . . . but maybe it was magic."

"How many other people were on the plane?"

Ty scrolled through the file and showed her a picture of a small, private airplane. "None. He was flying alone."

"No witnesses, then," Mira said.

"Maybe." Ty scrolled again, this time stopping on an address. "He flew out of a privately run airstrip, where he co-owned a plane with some friends. Maybe someone there can give us a clue as to what was going through our dead pilot's head before he jumped."

"Shouldn't we start with his family?"

Ty shrugged. "According to this, he didn't have any. Twenty-seven; lived alone; never married. His pilot friends are our best bet to find out what was eating at him and, hopefully, when and where his obsession started."

"Okay," she said. "To the airport." She jabbed him in the chest with her finger. "But let me know if your need to buy new shoes gets any stronger."

TWIN OAKS AIRPARK occupied sixty-five acres six miles south of Portland proper. Five long rows of hangars and fields with planes parked seemingly at random sat beside a cluster of more general-purpose buildings and a set of silos. The main office seemed to be a repurposed, two-story farmhouse surrounded by old-growth trees and lilac bushes. Half a dozen cars dotted the parking lot.

"How about I take the lead this time?" Mira said. "You just flash your badge and focus on staying sane."

Ty compressed his lips so tightly it looked as if it hurt, but he nodded.

A cool breeze lifted Mira's hair as she climbed the front steps, refreshing except for the scent of gasoline and engine oil. Opening the metal storm door rang a bell. Not a synthetic sound like the customer alert in the gas station, but a big brass bell that hung on a curved bar over the threshold. The office lobby was simple, practical, with a desk and chair on one side and a few more chairs on the other. Framed pictures and articles lined the walls—records of planes, pilots, and other notable history involving the airpark.

A man with wild white hair and more wrinkles than a raisin walked in from a back room. He rubbed his hands together and grinned. "Good afternoon. Are you here to schedule a flight? Or perhaps you're interested in getting your license?"

"Actually," Mira said, matching him grin for grin, "we're here to ask you about Dom Fischer."

Ty flashed his badge on cue, then put his hand in his pocket.

Mira knew Ty kept a good-luck charm in there that he claimed helped protect him from mental magics, although, when she'd snuck a peek awhile back, all she'd found was a rock. No magical properties at all.

<Relying on a rock to stay sane seems a bit like a child closing their eyes so the monsters can't see them,> the demon said derisively.

Mira brushed her fingers over the saint medallion hidden under her shirt. *His faith in the charm is what matters. Not the charm itself.*

<Whatever makes him feel better, I guess.>

The old man's expression snapped from gregarious to grief-stricken in no time flat. "Dom was a good guy. Got his license here about a year ago. Went in with some friends to buy a Cessna 150." He shook his head. "That boy loved to fly."

<Yeah, so much that he tried to do it without a plane.>

"Did you see him at all the day he died?" Mira asked.

"Nah. Despite what layfolk might think about air traffic regulations, private pilots pretty much come and go as they please. As long as they pay their hangar rent on time, we stay out of their hair." He scratched his head. "If you want to know more about Dom or what happened to him, talk to his buddy Jared in hangar twelve. I saw his truck in the lot earlier, so he should be around. He was the last one to interact with Dom before . . ." He trailed off and turned away.

"We'll do that," Mira said. "Thanks."

The hangars were numbered in red paint, so it didn't take long to find hangar twelve. The open doors revealed a wide space. No plane. A stocky man in his early thirties with spiked black hair and thick-framed glasses sat on a stool, idly swiveling back and forth. He was comfortably dressed in an open red flannel over a white shirt, blue jeans, and dark-brown work boots that had never seen a day of work. The only unkempt thing about him was a scabbed cut on his lower lip. He stared at a piece of metal cradled in his hands.

"Jared?" Mira asked, wishing she'd asked the old-timer for the man's last name.

Jared looked up. He frowned. "Can I help you?"

"I certainly hope so," she said. "We'd like to talk to you about your friend Dom Fischer."

His frown turned into a scowl. "I don't talk to reporters."

"We aren't reporters," Mira said. "We're with the PTF." She glanced at Ty, then nudged him in the ribs when he showed no sign of pulling out his badge.

Ty jerked, tearing his gaze away from Jared's boots.

<Kinky. I've never seen a person look at shoes with that kind of lust.> Despite the mocking playfulness of the comment, the demon sounded worried.

"Focus," Mira whispered out of the corner of her mouth, trying to keep her own concern in check. The best way to protect Ty was to get to the bottom of this curse . . . fast.

Ty flashed his badge, looking chagrined. "Williams and Fuentes. Sorry for your loss."

Jared pushed on the bridge of his glasses with one finger, sliding them higher up his nose. "I already told the police everything I know."

"Great," Mira said. "Now you can tell us."

Jared scowled. "Dom wasn't supposed to fly that day. I was on the roster."

"How many of you share the plane?"

"Six. We have an online sign-up sheet to prevent overlap. All the guys are local. We're friends. We met because we all came here for flight instruction when we were learning. Got our licenses around the same time. Decided to go in together on a plane, since that was about the only way any of us could afford it."

"So Dom broke protocol by coming here to fly that day without scheduling it first."

"Yeah. He got all up in my face, screaming about how he *had* to fly." Jared rubbed his thumb along the edge of the piece of metal he was holding, staring at it as though he could see the past reflected on the dull surface. "Normally I would have said 'fine, no big deal,' but I had actual plans that day. I was supposed to meet a friend. A . . . girl. I told him it was first come, first served on the roster. Aaand . . ."—he drew the word out—"he decked me."

"Hence the split lip," Mira said.

He snorted and nodded. "By the time I got off the floor, he was already in the plane."

"Had you noticed any odd behavior from him before that day? Any other unscheduled flights?"

"Honestly, our paths hadn't crossed in a while. We weren't even sure if he was going to stay in the group."

Mira frowned. "Why's that?"

"He was having trouble coming up with his share of the rent, paying for gas, all of it. Flying isn't a cheap hobby, and music teachers don't make a lot."

<Another human strapped for cash. Do any of you actually make enough to live off of?>

Very few. But that's not the point here. Dom didn't knock over a bank; he jumped out of an airplane. So it wasn't the money he was thinking about when he touched the coin. It was flying.

"Do you know where he went or what he did before he came here that day?"

"A pawnshop, I guess." Jared shrugged. "When Dom first came in, he told me he'd just pawned one of his guitars to cover the rent money he owed us. He tossed his coat and a bag of chips in a locker." He pointed to a set of three gray lockers next to a workbench at the back of the hangar. "Then he said he was going up. That's when we got in the fight."

<Doesn't sound like it was much of a fight,> the demon muttered.

"Mind if I take a look in the locker?" Mira asked.

"Be my guest." He waved her off and went back to staring at his piece of metal.

"What's that?" Ty asked, as Mira moved to check out the locker.

"A piece of the wreckage," Jared said in a hollow voice. "I should have tried harder to stop him."

"This isn't your fault," Ty said.

<Even cursed, he's much better at the people part of this job than you are.>

Whatever. Mira pulled open the locker. Resting on top of a half-empty bag of Cool Ranch Doritos were two crumpled receipts. The first was for the chips and an absent bottle of Coke, purchased from the grocery store where the cashier had died. The second was from a pawnshop, where Mr. Fischer had been paid six hundred dollars for a Fender Strat, less the cost of a *Tom Petty and the Heartbreakers Greatest Hits* album on vinyl, bringing the grand total to five hundred seventy-six dollars and thirty-seven cents—paid in cash.

"Those are nice boots," Ty said behind her as she looked over the store information on the pawnshop receipt. "What size are they?"

"Um, eleven."

"Perfect. Take them off."

<Uh oh.>

"What?" Jared chuckled halfheartedly, clearly thinking Ty was joking.

Coño. Mira pocketed the receipts and turned to see Jared fall off his stool with a yelp. Ty had his gun pointed straight at the poor man's chest.

<That guy's gonna piss himself.>

Can you blame him?

<Yep.>

"Ty," Mira called as she stepped toward him, hands raised. He didn't turn. "Ty, this isn't you. This is the curse. Remember Reyes. The shoes won't make you happy."

"I said take them off," Ty repeated.

<Does he even know we're here?>

I'm not sure. The curse is obviously driving him. Mira clenched her jaw. *I didn't expect him to flip this abruptly.*

Jared frantically tore at his laces, but he looked pleadingly at Mira. Tears leaked from his panicked eyes. "Do something!"

Mira took a few more steps, angling to get between the two men.

<You sure you wanna stand there? Ty isn't exactly thinking straight right now.>

Get ready to deflect the bullets if he shoots.

Mira summoned her own magic, practitioner magic, using the demon as fuel just as the demon had used her earlier.

"You don't want to do this, Ty." She was nearly between the two men. She kept her focus on Ty, though she was painfully aware of the human at her back and the fact that any flashy magic would give away what she was. *I'll bolster my strength and speed. Not enough for Mr. piss-pants to notice, but enough to give me the advantage in a fight.*

<So the plan is to whale on Ty till he cries for mercy?>

It sucks, but we have to get his mind off shoes.

<And if punching him isn't enough?>

He can't hurt anyone if he's unconscious. Including himself.

Ty shifted to keep the object of his obsession in sight as Mira threatened to block his view.

Using that moment when the gun was repositioning, Mira lunged. She cleared the space to Ty in one bound. The gun went off, but Mira had already grabbed Ty's wrists, redirecting the shot. The bullet pinged off the rafters and punched a hole in the tin roof.

"Get out of here!" she shouted over her shoulder as the momentum of her tackle carried her and Ty to the ground. Scuffs and a string of muttered curses trailed Jared across the room.

Mira rode Ty down and pinned his arms above his head. The gun went off again, tearing through the wall. Mira slammed Ty's hands into the concrete and forced his grip open, using her magic to overpower his normally superior strength. She knocked the gun away with a sound of scraping metal. No human could match a person amplified by magic, no matter how much bigger or stronger they were.

Ty growled and twisted, still trying to keep Jared in view as the terrified pilot ran from the hangar. Bucking his hips, he managed to roll Mira, but Mira planted her heels against Ty's thighs and kicked, reversing their positions again.

I can't let go long enough to hit him or he'll escape. Mira winced as Ty's knee slammed against her ribs. Pinning Ty's leg with her own, she made the decision she'd hoped to avoid. *Once the witness is clear, we'll drain Ty till he can't fight.*

Her mouth soured. The thought of taking Ty's energy against his will dragged Mira's mind to a darker place, to a time before she'd had full control of her powers and the demon's hunger had driven their every action . . . back when she'd killed more than just monsters.

Ty's head snapped up in a desperate headbutt that Mira barely managed to take on the cheek instead of the nose by twisting at the last moment. He snarled in her ear, sounding more like a wounded beast than a man.

<I have an idea.>

What?

<Let me through.> The demon flooded Mira's awareness, shoving her aside and taking control. Mira's mouth sealed over Ty's, forcing his head to the floor. His eyes went wide as Mira's tongue explored his lips.

Mira's reaction of *Are you insane?* petered out as Ty's mouth parted in response to her pressure. The growl changed in pitch, moving from anger to hunger. His arms relaxed, and the demon trailed Mira's hands down to his shoulders and up to his jaw. His hips and thighs moved against her, pulling her closer rather than pushing away. Strong hands caressed her back, sliding down to circle her waist.

Mira blinked and pulled back a fraction of an inch. "Why would you do that?" she whispered. She hadn't intended to say the words aloud. She only hoped they'd been too quiet for Ty to notice.

<Nothing gets a human's mind off, well . . . anything, better than sex.>

But—

<You didn't want to drain him without permission. Now you don't have to. You're welcome.>

Light and shadow played over Ty's too-close features through the curtain of Mira's hair. Hot breath warmed her face. The demon retreated, leaving her to face the fallout alone. She cleared her throat and sat up, straddling Ty's hips. Her muscles felt like jelly.

Ty stared at her with an expression somewhere between shock and awe, mouth still slightly open, eyes wide. Sweat glistened on his skin in echo of the heat flooding Mira's body.

"I, um . . ." She moved to get off him, but his grip held her in place. She gave him a stern look. "Let go."

"Why did you kiss me?"

She crossed her arms to cover the rise and fall of her faster-than-normal breathing as she tried to get her heart rate under control. "You were acting crazy." She frowned. "Don't you remember?"

His gaze grew distant and drifted to the side. "I remember talking to the dead pilot's friend . . . then everything gets a little hazy. You went to look in the lockers. My next clear thought . . ." His gaze snapped to Mira's mouth.

"You pulled your gun on our interviewee and demanded he take off his boots."

Ty groaned and covered his face with his hands. "Did I hurt him?"

"I tackled you, knocked the gun away—"

"And kissed me." He lowered his hands enough to look at her over his fingertips. She wasn't entirely sure what she saw in that gaze. Lust, certainly, but anger? Frustration? He liked the kiss, that much was clear from his reaction, but he wasn't entirely happy about it.

She pressed her lips together and stood. He didn't try to stop her this time. "We needed to get you thinking about something other than shoes." She walked over to Ty's gun and lifted it off the floor. "Maybe I should hang on to this for the time being."

He sat up and nodded. "Good idea." Rubbing one hand over his scalp he mumbled, "I could have killed an innocent man."

"But you didn't." Mira came closer and reached out to set her hand on his hunched back, but she stopped short of touching him and straightened. "You weren't in your right mind."

"And what about next time?" He twisted to look up at her. "This is only going to get worse."

"We'll take away your weapons and cuff your hands."

"Maybe we should lock me up . . . or sedate me in a hospital like the gas station clerk."

"We'll need the coin to break the curse once we find whoever set it loose, and you're the only one who can hold that without infecting more people." She gave him what she hoped was a comforting smile, though the distress she felt at seeing Ty lose his self-awareness to the curse was a restless beast tearing at her insides. She knew all too well the weight of harming innocents while out of control—knowing you weren't thinking straight didn't lessen the guilt. Eventually, the curse would direct that harm back on Ty. When that happened. . . . Mira shook her head. "I won't let you hurt *anyone*."

"Stopping me may take more than a kiss next time." The shadow of a smile tugged at his mouth but turned into a scowl. "You may have to put me down."

She shook her head. "It won't come to that."

"It might. Use whatever force you find necessary." He met her gaze. "I won't hold it against you."

A flutter of anxiety pinched Mira's chest. "Promise?"

This time he did smile. "I can't say I'll be happy about it . . . but I trust you. Do what you think is best."

She and Ty had struggled to establish a certain level of trust between them—especially in regards to her feeding, which he'd found repugnant when they first met. The fact that he was giving her a blank check to decide his fate meant more than she could say. "Deal," she said around the lump in her throat. She held her hand out to him, and, when he gripped it, she helped him up.

"So, what did you find in the locker?"

Chapter 7

Ty

TY TRIED TO ignore the furtive glances Mira kept casting his way as she drove to the address on the pawnshop receipt, as if worried he might make a grab for the steering wheel and send them careening in some undesired direction. He couldn't exactly blame her. Not after that affair in the hangar. Heat crept up his neck and seared his face. He closed his eyes and rubbed his forehead and temple with one hand, forced to lift the other as well by the handcuffs attached to his wrists. "If that man hasn't filed an assault charge with the police yet, he likely will soon."

"After he changes his pants," Mira muttered.

"This isn't funny, Mira. Once the police get involved, I'll have to explain that I've been magically compromised to avoid going to prison. Then the PTF will have no choice but to pull me off this case."

"They can't pull you. We have to break the curse."

"Protocols are protocols. An agent compromised by magic can't stay in the field. By all rights, I should be on my way to the field office right now to hand the case over to someone else."

"You can't possible think that someone else—"

"And I would be," he cut her off, "if not for you." He gave her a level look. "You're my best bet of living past tomorrow, so screw protocol." He cringed, imagining his boot camp drill sergeant glaring at him, as she had after every mistake, excuse, and practical joke gone wrong . . . right before assigning punishment. "I'm just saying, magical dementia aside, we don't have a lot of time before shit hits the fan."

"Then let's hope this pawnshop is our last stop." She pulled to the curb in front of a storefront with wide front windows screened by bars. The lights were off inside, and a red sign on the door read, *Sorry, we're closed.*

Ty frowned. "It's the middle of a weekday." He looked at the bustling shops on either side—a deli and an auto parts store. "Why would they be closed?"

"You sure the owner wasn't on your list of dead people?" Mira asked. "If they handled the coin . . ."

Ty pulled out his phone, not the easiest thing to do with his hands cuffed together, opened the files Kelley had sent, and passed the phone to Mira. "The heroin overdose was a teenager. Of the two gunshot victims, one was a housewife, the other was an accountant."

She scrolled as he spoke, then handed the phone back and said, "If no one died at this pawnshop, chances are good this is where the curse originated."

"Unless our dead pilot just picked the quarter up off the street somewhere."

"Glass half full," she chided, then she frowned. "Seriously though, why would a pawnshop owner want to curse a random customer?"

"Maybe he wasn't random," Ty said. "Maybe they have some other connection. I'll give Kelley a call while we have a look around, and see if he can dig anything up on the owner." He tipped his head toward the front door with its closed sign. "Can you get in there without making a scene?"

She raised an eyebrow.

"Right."

She twisted her lips to the side. "You wait here till I give the all-clear. I don't want you running after the first pair of Doc Martens to cross your path."

"That's not . . ." He shook his head and raised his hands. "Fine." He pointed to a surveillance camera mounted to the side of the building. "Mind the cameras, and check for alarms. We don't want to cross paths with the police any sooner than necessary."

She got out, circled the hood, and crossed the sidewalk to the pawnshop's front door, keeping half her attention on him the whole time. She made a show of looking in the shop window as a few pedestrians passed. Ty glanced at their footwear, then quickly away before he could register the details.

Seriously. Shoes. Of all the lame-ass obsessions to be done in by . . . He wanted to laugh, but the seriousness of his situation, no matter how ridiculous, turned all levity sour.

Once the sidewalk was clear, Mira took hold of the pawnshop's doorknob. There was no noticeable change in her, but a moment later she twisted the knob and pushed the door open. Magic was funny like that. Sometimes it was all fireworks and spectacle; other times it was a flipped switch, or a dented quarter. The world had become a very strange place in the last twenty years. Or maybe it had always been strange, and he only noticed more now.

Mira glanced up and down the street, then waved for him to join her.

He fumbled with the truck's door, slid out, and hustled into the pawnshop, doing his best to mask his metal bracelets with his hands and body.

This is humiliating, he thought as he breached the dim interior of the pawnshop. *If anyone sees me like this, they'll assume I'm some kind of criminal.* He thought of the man in the airplane hangar. He couldn't remember clearly what he'd done, but the handcuffs suddenly felt appropriate. He glanced around the pawnshop. Shelves of books, movies, music, and other stackable items filled half the store. The other half catered to larger items, such as computers, power tools, sports equipment, and musical instruments. Long glass cabinets at the far end of the shop held jewelry, smaller electronic devices, collectibles—including a handful of antique coins—and a few guns. *Please let this be the source of the curse.*

Mira pushed past him, closing and locking the door behind her. She crossed the *Employees only* barrier that granted access to the area behind the glass counters. "I'm not picking up any magic in here."

Ty spotted two more security cameras and pointed them out to Mira. "There should be a computer recording all the footage from these cameras. Let's check the back."

He led the way through an arched opening behind the counter that led to a second, smaller room cluttered with what looked to be overstock. A three-drawer filing cabinet and a rolltop desk occupied a clear space against one wall. Mounted above the desk was a monitor displaying a quartered screen. Each of the four frames showed a different angle on the store—the front door, the main area, the counter, and the back room. Ty saw the back of his head on the screen, turned, and found the corresponding camera mounted high in the corner.

Mira sat down at the desk, which housed a keyboard and mouse that, presumably, connected to the security system. "Dom Fischer's receipt puts him at the pawnshop four days ago. I'll start there and work my way backward while you call Kelley and find out why there's nobody here."

Nodding, Ty pulled his phone out of his pocket, placed the call, and raised it to his ear, all while moving both hands in tandem. *This is going to get very old very quickly*, he thought as he waited for the call to connect.

"Do you have an update, Agent Williams?" Kelley's voice was tired but eager.

"We're making progress," Ty said. "I need you to check the system for anything on the owner of Prize Pawn on Seventeenth Street."

"Just a second."

Ty paced the claustrophobic space of the storage room, eyes roving the piles of miscellanea. He caught a glimpse of a pair of dark-brown

Park Avenue Oxfords similar to the ones he was currently wearing, minus the hole, tucked away on a high shelf. *Those are nice.* Sweat broke out on his palms. His pulse pounded in his ears.

"Oh, shit," Kelley said.

Ty tore his gaze away from the shoes with difficulty. "What is it?"

"She's dead."

His gaze drifted back to the Oxfords. *I wonder if they're my size?*

Shaking his head, he turned his back on the shoes and lowered the phone so that he could dig the stone out of his pocket. Clutching the stone in one hand, he took a deep breath and lifted the phone to his ear. "The pawnshop owner is dead?" He glanced at Mira, but she was absorbed in her own work, squinting at the monitor as it raced backward through time. "Why wasn't she on the list you sent earlier?"

"That list only covered deaths in Portland. She died in California. Took a turn too fast on Highway One and landed her Porsche at the bottom of a cliff, after amassing an impressive number of speeding tickets between here and there."

Frustration and dread welled up inside Ty, threatening to overwhelm him. If the pawnshop owner was dead, they couldn't have been the source of the curse.

"Does he look familiar to you?" Mira mumbled.

Startled out of his thoughts by the randomness of her question, Ty stepped closer and studied the screen over Mira's shoulder, unsure which "he" she was referring to, as she rewound and played back a section of the recording.

"Don't be an ass," she said.

Ty stiffened then realized Mira wasn't talking to him at all, but to the demon inside her. Usually she kept such conversations contained to the privacy of her thoughts, but sometimes she spoke out loud. It could be . . . unsettling. Especially when he was already having a second conversation on the phone.

"You're right." She froze the playback on a frame of a boy's face, twisted around, and jumped to find Ty staring at her. She hesitated then pointed at the screen. "Isn't this the kid from the overdose case on your death list?"

"Hang on, Kelley." Still clutching his anchor stone in three fingers on his right hand, Ty swiped the call to the background, opened the overdose file, and compared the customer on the security footage to the picture of the corpse from the police report. White-blond hair, pale complexion, bony cheeks, and a dark mole or freckle on the right side of his narrow jaw. He was a perfect match.

"This kid is listed as a John Doe," Ty said, skimming the rest of the report. "The time stamp on this footage is barely two hours before his estimated time of death."

"Guess we know how he spent his money," Mira said. "And check this out." She set the video in motion again. The pawnshop owner, a tall woman with long, dark hair and a hooked beak of a nose, sorted through the pile of jewelry the boy had dumped on the counter with speedy precision. Halfway through sorting, she lifted a small, circular object and handed it back to the boy with a shake of her head. The boy looked at the rejected item, shrugged, and inserted it into an antique gumball machine beside the register. He twisted the device, retrieved his prize, and popped the ball into his mouth.

"Do you think . . .?" Ty licked his lips, unwilling to get his hopes up.

"Let's check." Mira paused the video again and led the way back to the front of the shop. She examined the gumball machine, a pewter stand with a large glass dome filled with colored candies. "It takes quarters," she said with a smile. She turned the device around and pointed out a small lock on the back.

"What's going on?" Kelley's voice drifted faintly out of Ty's phone.

"Hang on," Ty said again. He set the phone on the counter, stuffed his river rock back in his pocket, and rummaged through the odds and ends behind the counter, coming up with a tiny silver key that looked just the right size for the gumball lock. He handed the key to Mira.

She opened the machine and looked inside. "Empty."

"So the kid buys a gumball with the cursed coin. The owner empties her proceeds into the register then hands off the quarter as part of the payment when the broke pilot pawns his guitar."

"But the coin was mixed in with that jewelry," Mira said. "I don't think the kid knew it was there until the clerk handed it back to him."

"That's quite the jewelry collection for a teenage boy." Ty lifted his phone and said, "Kelley, have there been any recent thefts in the area involving jewelry?"

Kelley hummed as he searched police reports. "Just one. An elderly woman in an apartment building on Eighth Street. Apparently someone took over twelve hundred dollars' worth of jewelry from her bedroom while she was out for a walk."

"Text me her address," Ty said. "And a list of the stolen items, if you have it."

Ty hung up and searched the shelves behind and under the counter near the register. "Ah ha." He slapped a thick receipt book down on the glass countertop. A niggling prickle on the back of his neck made him look toward the back room. His phone chimed. Kelley had sent the requested information.

Shaking his head, Ty flipped through the receipt book to the day timestamped on the surveillance video. He trailed his finger over pink carbon copy slips full of cramped script. Stopping on a set of descriptions involving gold and gems, he compared the pawned items to the list from the theft report Kelley had sent. He tapped his index finger next to the name on the receipt. "Steven Carter."

"That's probably John Doe's alias," Mira said, crossing her arms.

"Here." He passed the list to Mira. "See if you can find all the items that kid pawned. There's one more thing I need to check."

Mira took the list, opened the glass case housing the store's jewelry, and began matching descriptions to their physical counterparts.

Ty returned to the storage room, following the nagging whisper at the back of his mind that insisted he'd left something undone. Something important. He cast one hesitant glance at Mira, then turned his focus to the brown Oxfords on their shelf. He swallowed and wiped his sweaty palms against his thighs. *I just want to know if they fit. Nothing wrong with that. I need a new pair anyway, and they're here. It's not like I won't pay for them.*

He looked around for a step stool but, not finding one, ended up climbing the metal shelves. The freestanding structure wobbled under his weight. A shiny poison-green bowling ball rolled dangerously close to the edge, bumping his fingers. Reaching up, he grabbed the shoes and jumped down. The bowling ball teetered and fell. It hit the floor with a solid *thunk* that left a dent in the synthetic wood next to Ty's foot then rolled away, seeking the lowest point in the room.

Ty cradled the Oxfords to his chest with a smile. He dropped where he stood, landing hard on his butt, and ripped off the offensive shoe with the hole in its side, thinking, *These will be so much better. Clean. Respectable. This is how a man should dress.*

He loosened the laces on the shoe that matched his sock-covered foot and shoved his toes inside. His foot slammed to a halt with the heel still out.

Grimacing, he pushed harder, trying to force his foot into the too-small shoe. He bit his lower lip and curled his toes, but his heel remained exposed.

No, he thought. *These shoes are perfect. I just need . . .* He looked around for something sharp enough to remove the troublesome toes.

Chapter 8

Mira

MIRA PAWED through gold chains, emerald earrings, opal brooches, and diamond bracelets, looking for the perfect matches to the items on Ty's list. Items that had been stolen and wrapped in a bundle alongside a dangerously inconspicuous coin.

<Ooh, I like that red one.> The demon moved Mira's hand toward a ruby pendant hanging from a gold chain.

Mira curled her fingers short of touching the precious gem. "That one's not on the list."

<So?>

"So taking that one would be stealing." Mira picked up a pearl choker and added it to the growing pile on top of the counter.

<So?> the demon repeated. <You've stolen things before.>

"Things I needed. Things like food."

<And money.>

"To buy things like food."

<You'd look great in that necklace.>

"Doesn't matter."

<Ty would like it.>

"Still doesn't matter." She sifted through a tray of rings. "We're looking for a ring with a 'plant-themed band and cushion-cut citrine.' What do you suppose a citrine looks like?"

The demon shrugged. <Not as pretty as a ruby?>

Mira lifted a gold ring with a yellow, rectangular gem in a setting cast to resemble leaves and a band of twisting vines. "Apparently they're yellow."

A muffled thud came from the back room. She looked toward the opening. "You okay in there?" She waited for a response, anxiety mounting. "Ty?"

A low muttering emanated from the back room.

<That's not a good sign.>

Setting the ring on top of her pile, Mira stood and walked to the storage area. A bowling ball bumped the side of her foot, then rolled past into the store proper. Ty stood with one bare foot propped on top of the desk. His damp sock draped the security monitor. He raised his arms. Both his hands were wrapped around the hilt of a long, slightly curved sword with a dragon etched along the silvery length of the blade.

"*Coño,*" Mira swore as she lunged across the room, grabbing Ty's wrists as the sword began its downward arc. "Ty!" she screamed in his face. "What on God's green Earth do you think you're doing?"

He blinked and frowned. "I just need to make a little adjustment."

"To your foot?"

He nodded and turned his head. She followed his gaze to a pair of brown shoes on the storeroom floor. "They don't fit."

The demon gave a soft whistle. <That is some serious devotion to fashion.>

That's the curse turning his brain to mush, Mira corrected, furious at herself for letting Ty out of her sight, even for a moment. She wasn't used to, or cut out for, this type of constant worrying about another person. To Ty she said, "I know how to make the shoes fit."

"Really?" His eyes lit up.

"Really," she said. "And I'll tell you, but first you have to give me the sword."

He lowered his arms, bringing the hilt within reach.

<This might backfire when he realizes you can't actually make his big-ass feet fit in those tiny shoes.>

Mira peeled Ty's fingers off the sword. He didn't resist. She tossed the blade out of reach. "Good. Now we just need one more thing."

Ty waited placidly, eyes full of trust.

Mira took a breath and, holding Ty's gaze, shoved her hand in the right-side pocket of his pants.

<Damn, girl!>

Shut up. She pushed past a set of keys.

<Is that the pocket he put the coin in?>

Mira froze, replaying the scene in the hospital room. He'd put the coin in an evidence bag, and she didn't feel any plastic. *I think that went in the left pocket.*

<Then what are you looking for?>

She curled her fingers around a smooth, oval object at the bottom of Ty's pocket. The stone was warm. It didn't weigh a lot, but it had a solid presence. She could see why Ty found it comforting.

"Hold out your hand," Mira said.

He did as instructed.

She set the river rock on the center of his palm. It was a gray so dark it was almost black, with specks that made it resemble the night sky. A long fissure marred one side, though the edges had been worn smooth from years of handling.

Ty frowned. He started to turn, to look toward the shoes. "I don't see how this will—"

Mira pressed her hand to his cheek and forced his attention back to her. "Look at me." She set her other hand against his other cheek, trapping his face. "We're going to do some magic, but you have to do what I say, or the magic won't work."

His frown deepened. A ridge folded between his eyebrows as the waves of his confused thoughts crashed against reality.

"Do you trust me, Ty?" Mira held her breath.

Ty's forehead smoothed. "Of course. You're my partner."

"Good. Then do as I say. I'm going to make sure you get exactly what you need." She reached down and cupped her fingers around Ty's, closing his hands over the stone. "Close your eyes."

He gave her a suspicious look, then did as instructed.

Sliding the hand that still cupped his cheek along his jaw until her fingertips reached the buzzed fluff at the base of his skull, she tipped his head down so that his forehead rested against hers. Their breath mingled.

Ty's frown came back. "I really don't see how—"

"Shh," Mira said. "You need to focus on the rock in your hand." She squeezed the hand cradling the stone, forcing his attention there.

"What does a rock have to do with my shoes?"

"If you want to get what you need, this is the way. Trace the curves. Recreate the rock in your mind. When you're not thinking about anything but that rock, the magic will work."

He exhaled, stirring the hair around Mira's face. His hands moved under hers, turning the stone over, tracing the old wound with his thumb. The handcuffs connecting his wrists rattled and clanked as they bumped together.

<What exactly is this supposed to accomplish?>

Not all magic comes from the Rift. "Remember the rock," Mira said in a soothing whisper. She matched Ty's breathing. On the next exhale she said, "Remember every time you've held it." Inhale. "Remember what it means to you."

On the following exhale Ty whispered, "Stay in the moment." His eyes flickered open. Molten chocolate stared into Mira's soul. "Mira."

She swallowed the butterflies suddenly trying to erupt from her throat and searched his expression. He didn't *look* crazy anymore. "Are you . . . okay?"

He nodded, brushing the tip of her nose with his. "It's weird, but from the second I looked at those shoes—"

He started to turn, or maybe just to gesture, but Mira clamped her hands to either side of his head and brought him back to center. "Stay with me."

"I'm fine," he said. "Present." He took a deep breath and stepped back, breaking her hold. "Everything's sort of . . . foggy, but whatever I was doing . . . it seemed to make so much sense at the time."

"Trust me, it didn't."

<Yeah, he's totally crazy pants.>

He looked down and rolled the non-magic stone that had just performed a miracle across his palm. "You didn't kiss me this time."

She grinned. "Disappointed?"

One corner of his mouth quirked up. "Maybe a little."

Mira nearly choked.

The demon came to attention. <Now we're talkin'.>

Ty cleared his throat with a hasty wave of dismissal. "Kidding. Just . . . this is better."

"Right," Mira said, fighting for balance in the tornado of emotions his wayward comment had caused. Her mind circled back to Lisa and Antony, who'd destroyed both their marriages for a hotel tumble. She set her jaw. "We're partners."

"Totally platonic," Ty confirmed.

<Ugh!> the demon groaned with the mental equivalent of a facepalm.

Mira had no intention of ruining the partnership she had with Ty, so why did his agreement feel like getting hit by a train? "Come on." She grabbed Ty's sock off the monitor and turned him bodily toward the arch leading to the main shop, pushing from behind so he wouldn't see her disappointment. "I'm almost done sorting out the stolen jewelry. You can sit with your eyes closed and fondle your rock while I finish."

Ty grimaced. "Great."

Cradling his anchor stone between his palms like a sacred relic, Ty read entries off the police report while Mira located the remainder of the stolen jewelry. It seemed none had been sold off yet.

"That's all of it," Ty said.

Setting an opal brooch on top of the pile, Mira placed her hands on her hips.

The demon made a *hmm* noise that buzzed like a bee in Mira's mind. <Where's a shoebox when you need one?>

Don't even joke about that!

<I just meant we need a way to carry all this stuff.>

Mira overturned one of the velvet-lined trays in the display cabinet, dumping its remaining contents in a heap on the wooden shelf. *Problem solved.*

"If the coin was nicked along with the jewels," Ty said, "there's a good chance the old lady who filed the police report is a fae. An unregistered fae, since there was no mention of magical heritage."

"Which means she won't be happy to see the PTF on her doorstep," Mira said, lifting the tray of recovered jewelry. "I suggest you let *me* take the lead this time. Keep your badge in your pocket."

Ty shook his head. "Brute force isn't the answer to everything. The threat of deportation should give us enough leverage to make the fae cooperate without risk of a firefight."

"Or she'll take one look at your badge and blow your head off," Mira countered.

"In which case you have permission to save my ass and spend the rest of our lives rubbing it in that I was wrong."

Mira grinned. "Deal."

Ty led the way out of the shop, hands clamped around his rock.

Mira cast one last look at the storage room, remembering the way her heart had leapt into her throat at the sight of Ty wielding that sword, intent on mutilating himself. The sour flavor came back to her mouth. *This fae better be able to fix him.* Shaking her head, she stepped outside and pulled the door with its *closed* sign shut behind her.

Burnt-orange light dulled the corners of the world and turned the underbelly of the cloud-strewn sky into a tie-dyed riot as Mira drove to the address listed on the police report. More than half a day had passed since Ty touched the cursed coin in Matthew Clark's hospital room. The longest they knew for certain someone had survived after contracting the curse was a day and a half, and only because he'd been sedated. Most of the victims died within hours. She tightened her grip on the steering wheel.

<He'll be fine,> the demon said. <Worst case, we'll keep him weak as a kitten and chained to a bed until we get to the bottom of this, so he can't do anything reckless.>

"We don't know how the enchantment works. Maybe if it can't get people to kill themselves after two days it explodes their heart or something."

"What?" Ty's wide, worried gaze swung in her direction.

Shit! Did I say that out loud?

<You know I can't tell.>

She kept her focus on the stop-and-go traffic that kept her from racing to her destination. "I was just thinking out loud."

"And you think the curse has a second stage that could kill a person directly if the whole suicidal obsession thing fails to do the job?"

She trapped her lower lip between her teeth and didn't answer.

"Great." He tipped his head back and closed his eyes, hands clasped as if in prayer around the tiny pebble of sanity trapped between his palms.

Long shadows stretched between blazing rooftops as the sun sank toward the ocean in the west. Mira pulled to the curb in front of a five-story, stucco building with barred windows. She glanced at Ty. He rocked gently on the seat, knuckles white. His eyes darted back and forth, tracking each pedestrian on the surrounding sidewalks.

". . . never going to take me seriously," he muttered.

His sock-clad foot sat in stark contrast to his remaining shoe. Mira hadn't dared go back for the one with the hole. Not only hadn't she wanted to leave Ty alone for even a moment, she couldn't be sure seeing the offending shoe wouldn't send him spiraling into another episode. Staring at his mismatched footwear, she wasn't sure this was better.

". . . look ridiculous." A muscle in Ty's cheek twitched, making him look even more insane when coupled with his random mutterings.

<Maybe we should just knock him out and leave him here. We can lock him in the back so no one sees him.>

What if he wakes up? Mira countered. She looked to the fourth floor of the building. *What if the fae we need is sitting in that room up there, but we don't have the coin with us when we knock, and she gets away before we can drag her out to Ty?*

A sudden gust of wind brought Mira's rambling thoughts to a halt as Ty exited the truck.

She reached for the tray of stolen jewelry, which they'd planned on Ty carrying to keep Mira's hands free in case this house call turned into a fight. "Don't forget—"

But Ty was gone, off and running up the street.

"*Coño!*" She scrambled over the seat and out Ty's still-open door, slamming it behind her.

Ty's long legs gobbled up the pavement as he sprinted ahead, barreling through anyone unfortunate enough to cross his path. Shouts and curses followed in his wake.

Mira poured magic into her limbs, strengthening her muscles and reinforcing her lungs. She sprang forward at Olympic speed, hurdling a man in a navy-blue overcoat whom Ty had knocked to the ground. The smell of car exhaust filled Mira's nostrils and stung the back of her throat. She pumped her arms, gaining ground.

Ty flew across the street at the end of the block without pause. Tires screeched. Horns blared. Headlights flashed in Mira's periphery as her sneakers pounded damp asphalt to the beat of her frantic pulse.

<We were literally seconds away from a possible solution . . . and he pulls this?>

He can't help it. Even Mira's internal voice sounded winded as she pushed herself to run faster.

<Where is he even going?>

But Mira was too focused to answer. Acid burned in her veins as her muscles started to cramp. Magic could push her past her limits. That didn't mean there wasn't a cost. She clenched her jaw against the pain building in her side. Ty was almost within reach.

Ty sprinted into the next river of asphalt as headlights swung across Mira's vision, blinding her. She lunged forward, catching Ty around the shoulders and carrying them both forward with her momentum. Gasps and shouts echoed around them as a silver minivan plowed through the space they'd just vacated and screeched to a halt. Her shoulder slammed into the ground with Ty on top of it, and the two of them rolled over.

Ty grunted but immediately tried to scramble up.

<No you don't!> The demon tugged Ty's life force through Mira's grip. His knees turned to liquid, dropping him back to the ground like a puppet with its strings cut.

Mira cradled the side of Ty's face, searching his gaze for some sign of awareness, and whispered, "I'm so sorry."

<He'll forgive you,> the demon said. <Heck, he already gave you permission. Any means necessary, right?>

Mira cringed as the demon siphoned off more energy, careful not to disturb the flows tainted with fae magic. Even so, Mira wanted to puke.

The demon was right. Ty had given her permission. She wasn't draining him against his will. So why did she still feel so crappy about doing it? *Because this is what makes me a monster,* she thought. *This is, and always will be, my life. Draining energy from others, whether humans or rifters.* Without that constant influx of energy, Mira's demon would burn her body to ash within months—the ultimate fate of every rifter. *I can never have a normal life.*

She stiffened. That thought had surprised her, but not because she hadn't realized the truth before. She'd given up any semblance of a normal life ages ago. At least, she thought she had. No, what surprised her was the germ of sadness she'd felt—a feeling that said she'd dared to hope, that somewhere in the past few months she'd started thinking her life might take a different path. But that was impossible. There was no different path for her. No normal. People like Ty could wear the badge, do the job, then retire. Mira was a warrior of God. She *was* the job, and she couldn't put that down until she was dead. There could be no "happily ever after" for someone like her.

The flow of energy trickled away. Ty's head rocked fitfully from side to side for a moment as a final muttered worry tumbled from his lips, then he was still. His chest rose and fell in deep, even breaths.

<He'll be fine in a few hours,> the demon assured.

Assuming we've found a way to break the curse by then.

<Obviously.>

Mira took comfort from the demon's self-assured tone, as if there could be no doubt that they would succeed.

"Are you two all right?"

Mira twisted to find the owner of the deep voice. A man in scuffed work boots, brown corduroy pants, a Grateful Dead T-shirt, and a brown leather jacket was standing in front of the open driver's-side door of the minivan. Startled eyes stared from deep-set sockets in a pale face framed by shoulder-length brown hair.

"He just jumped out," the man said, waving his hands to indicate Ty, whose unconsciousness the driver probably feared was his own fault. "He came out of nowhere, and just—"

"It's fine." Mira sat up as she spoke. Another round of gasps and mutters rippled through the gathered onlookers. The driver who'd almost hit them jerked as though recoiling from an open flame. She followed the man's gaze to the metal cuffs around Ty's wrists.

Crap.

<Just tell them you're a cop in pursuit of a fleeing criminal. It's not that far off.>

Except for the part about Ty being a criminal.

<He did try to shoot a guy for his shoes earlier today,> the demon pointed out.

Mira slid her hand surreptitiously into Ty's pocket, rolling him just enough to get his weight off that side, and grabbed the leather wallet that held his badge. With a sick twisting in her gut at making Ty out to be the bad guy, she pretended to draw the badge from her own pocket and flashed it around, careful not to show the picture part of his ID. "Official PTF business." She spoke with the authority of someone used to being obeyed.

Everyone on the street took a collective inhale and a hasty step back, as if the mere mention of magic might somehow contaminate them. With that one lie, the expressions focused on Ty morphed from concern and curiosity to fear and suspicion—looks Mira knew all too well.

"Do you want me to call an ambulance?" the driver asked. "Or the police?"

Mira cleared her throat, trying to dislodge the boulder that had appeared there. She didn't like drawing attention even at the best of times, which this definitely was not. She certainly didn't want anyone official taking notice of this event. "I've got this under control." She gestured back the way they'd come. "My vehicle is just up the street."

She stood up, tucked Ty's PTF badge in her own pocket, and looked down at her prone partner. *Damn it, Ty! You couldn't hold it together for five more minutes?*

She noticed a smooth black stone with a scratch on the top lying on the sidewalk next to Ty's limp fingers. Frowning, she picked up the stone and put that in her pocket as well.

"Do you need"—the driver swallowed, hesitating, then finally spit out the last word with a wince—"help?"

She looked again at the gathered crowd, still keeping their distance. She'd be lucky if one of them didn't try to slide a knife in Ty's back just to rid the world of one more magic user.

<Oh, the irony.>

She lifted a placating hand. "I've got this."

She stared down at Ty's limp form and pursed her lips. The stitch in her side had dulled with the infusion of Ty's energy—a good thing, since she now had to cover the same distance again, this time with Ty's added weight. At least she didn't have to run. Sighing, she once more bolstered her muscles with magic.

<You sure you want to do that? We may have a fight with a fae at the end of this walk. Maybe we should save our energy.>

I'll only use what I absolutely need. A boost to get him on my back shouldn't take much.

Mira grabbed Ty's handcuffed wrists and pulled him into a sitting position. Ducking under the circle of his arms, she pressed her back to the warmth of his chest, wrapped one arm around his muscular thigh while pinning his shoulder with the other, and heaved to her feet, lifting him in a fireman's carry. She wobbled as his weight settled, bending her nearly double as she tried to balance the load.

Ugh, why does he have to weigh so much?

<Because he's a sexy six feet of pure muscle?>

The driver reached out a tentative hand. "Are you sure you don't want—"

"I'm fine," she snapped. Then said in a slightly more even tone, "Just move along."

Phones flashed and Mira's cheeks burned as onlookers snapped pictures and tittered behind their hands.

Of all the ridiculous, mortifying . . . Mira took one tentative step, then another. Even with the thread of magic running through her body, she had difficulty balancing Ty's awkward mass as she moved.

She chafed under the scandalized stares that followed her down the street. Halfway along the block, a young woman stepped out of a cab in front of her and stopped in her tracks, jaw dropping and eyes going wide. Mira forced a grin, said, "Couldn't hold his liquor," and hurried past as fast as her ponderous gait would take her.

She could feel the demon struggling to suppress its laughter as she caught sight of her reflection in the mirrored windows of a coffee shop. She was nearly invisible beneath Ty's bulk. Her slender arm wrapped a thigh the size of her waist. Hunched as she was, his toes nearly scraped the ground while her spindly legs moved under him. Merged in the reflection, they looked like some grotesquely mutated spider creeping down the road.

Focusing on the sidewalk in front of her and the apartment near where her truck was parked, she placed one foot in front of the other. *Almost there.*

<Then what?> asked the demon. <We can't exactly fight a fae with Ty on your back.>

"I'm hoping we won't have to fight," she said through gritted teeth.

<Yeah, but how often does that work out?>

"Maybe the fae will be so grateful to get her coin back that she'll release Ty and Matthew from the curse as thanks."

<Because we've met so many kind and grateful fae,> scoffed the demon. <More likely she'll try to kill us, too, for uncovering her secret identity.>

"She reported the jewelry missing," Mira reasoned. "If she didn't want the coin back, she would have kept her mouth shut about the theft."

<But she didn't report the coin,> the demon countered, <or warn the police about its lethal affects.>

Mira hesitated. "Fine. We'll assume we're about to knock on the door of a dangerous fae with nefarious plans to wipe out the human race one obsessive fool at a time." She glanced at Ty's slack features. "No offense."

<In which case we'll probably need to beat her into submission to get her to lift the curse.>

Mira wrestled with the door to the apartment with one hand while trying not to drop Ty or fall over. A few people threw glances in her direction, but no one offered to open the damn door.

<Aren't you going to bring the stolen jewelry up with you?>

"And how exactly do you propose I carry those when I've got my hands full with Ty?" She said through gritted teeth. "The coin is more important. We can return the jewelry after the curse is lifted."

<Are we starting with offense or defense?> the demon asked.

"Defense." Mira grunted, finally wedging herself and Ty's much larger frame through the opening. "She can't break the curse if she's dead." She stumbled along yellowed linoleum, nose burning from the scent of "lemony-fresh" cleaner, past a bank of brass mailboxes, to an elevator beside a set of stairs. A paper sign was duct taped across the doors. *Out of service.*

She stared at the sign. "You have got to be fucking kidding me."

Chapter 9

Mira

MIRA KNELT AND let Ty slide to the thin carpeting on the fourth-floor landing, careful that he didn't bang his head. She shivered as air reached her sweat-soaked shirt where Ty's body had been pressed against hers. Her chest heaved. Her legs wobbled as she sat down to catch her breath, releasing the trickle of energy that had kept her from collapsing under Ty's weight.

<Maybe you should have used more magic,> the demon said.

Mira scowled. *You're the one who pointed out that we might need to fight a fae at the end of this walk.*

<That was before I realized what a wimp you are. I thought you were in good shape for a human.>

Mira gestured to Ty's unconscious form and hissed, "He's twice the size of me."

<So?>

Mira rolled her eyes. Trying to explain the concept of mass to an incorporeal being was a quick trip to a headache, and she already had one of those. "Let's just find this fae, so Ty can walk out of here on his own two feet."

The police report listed the owner of the stolen jewelry as an eighty-year-old woman named Olivia Bransen, who lived in apartment 4b. Mira looked down the wood-paneled hall, glancing at the black letters painted next to each of the four doors. 4b was second on the right. Straightening, she gripped Ty's forearms above his handcuffed wrists and dragged him over the compressed, gray carpet until they were within a foot of the target door.

Ready?

<Always.>

Taking a deep breath, Mira called up her magic once more, dropped into a defensive stance, and knocked.

The door swung open about four inches, and a pair of brown eyes marred by a milky-white fog peeked out. The woman on the other side of the threshold matched Mira's petite five-feet-four-inch stature, but probably stood taller in her younger years, when the bow of her back was not so pronounced. A scaffold of buried beauty supported layers of freckled skin that folded like fabric. Fine threads of silvery moonbeams cascaded over her scalp and shoulders. Pink paisley terrycloth wrapped the woman's frail frame down to varicose ankles and faded pink slippers, which were decorated with floppy felt ears, button eyes, and embroidered noses bordered by mangled wire whiskers.

Mira kept her guard up. The woman's ancient appearance could easily be a glamour, and age didn't mean the same thing when the fae were involved. The longer they lived, the stronger they grew.

<Definitely fae,> the demon confirmed, <but barely enough to register. Probably some bastard offspring from twenty generations ago. No way is she the one who enchanted that coin.>

Mira's heart sank. She needed answers. Ty didn't have time for a dead end. *Do you think she even knows about the curse? Or what she is, for that matter? She wouldn't be the first halfer kept in the dark about their lineage.*

<If that were the case, why was the coin with her jewelry and not in her piggy bank?>

Good point. Mira felt her spirits lift. *Even if she didn't cast the curse, she may still know how to break it. And a hidden halfer means Ty's straightforward PTF approach should work. No fighting necessary.*

<Boooooring,> the demon sing-songed.

But effective, Mira countered. *Right now, that's all that matters.*

"Can I help you?" The irritated tone of the woman's gravelly voice belied the hospitality of her words.

"I've recovered some jewelry that I believe was stolen from you," Mira said. "I've come to return your possessions."

"Oh." Suspicion morphed into surprise, then wariness, on the woman's face. Her gaze skittered away from Mira's, flitting up and down the hall. She caught sight of Ty, unconscious on the floor, and sucked in a sharp inhale.

"*All* of your possessions," Mira said with emphasis. "Including a rather unique coin." She pulled Ty's badge from her pocket.

The cataract stare widened further as it shot back to Mira and the PTF badge. The woman's face twisted in fear. She tried to slam the door, but Mira wedged her foot against the frame. She shoved the door open, stepping through the gap as the elderly woman stumbled back.

"Get out of my home!" the woman shrieked. "Help! Help!"

"Are you sure you want to do that?" Mira asked. "Because your name didn't come up on the registry, and possession of magical artifacts is kind of a big deal."

The woman's papery lips snapped closed. She swallowed, pulled her robe tighter, then lifted her chin. "I have no idea what you're talking about."

"You're a terrible liar," Mira said. Stepping back into the hall, she glanced up and down the dimly lit corridor. None of the other doors had opened at the woman's cries. With a burst of magical strength, she hoisted Ty by his shoulders, dragged him over the threshold, and deposited him on a woven rug in the main room of the eclectically furnished apartment. A single bedroom and a bathroom opened off the central area, which served as living room, dining room, and kitchen all rolled into one. She cast one last look into the empty hall, then closed the door to grant them privacy for what came next.

The old woman watched the production without a word, but the constant shifting of her eyes and the way she clutched her robe gave away her unease.

Mira leveled her gaze at the unregistered fae halfer. "Look, I'm not here to cause you any trouble. I don't care if you're registered or not. I'm just here to return your property and get you to set things right."

"What makes you think I want it back?"

Mira frowned. "You reported the theft."

The old woman grunted and settled into a straight-backed wooden chair beside an oak table with a million tiny scars across its surface. "Then I had a few days to think about the situation, and do you know what I realized?" She leveled her cataract stare at Mira. "I don't owe anything to anyone. Not the bitch fae who dumped that curse on my family and disappeared. Not your self-righteous agency that would have arrested me for possessing an illegal magical artifact if I'd dared to register as a halfer. That damned coin ruined my life. I never asked for any of this—the isolation, the responsibility, the fear. I never wanted to be a guardian. I've been trapped since the day that coin came to me, but no more. I'm finally free of it, and I don't want it back."

Frustration warred with empathy, boiling beneath Mira's skin. She knew what it was to be marked by magic. She knew how it felt to have any chance of a normal life stripped away . . . to live in the shadows, hiding what she was from friends and enemies alike, while the rest of the world basked in the sun. She could sympathize with this woman's choice to let the world that rejected her fend for itself, but she couldn't accept it. Not when Ty's life was on the line. She balled her fists. She had to snap this woman out of her self-pity and convince her to help break the curse.

"You think you're the only one screwed over by fate? You think you're the only person who didn't get to live the life they wanted? Who had their choices stolen away by powers outside of their control?" She took a deep, shaky breath. "Like it or not, you *do* have a responsibility here. You're the one who let this curse off its leash. You need to help me fix this mess."

"Or what? You'll lock me up? You'll kill me?" The woman gave a brittle laugh. "Go ahead. I'm old. I have cancer in my liver. I'll be dead soon anyway. I plan to go out on my own terms, not shackled to the magic that ruined my life."

"But . . . people are *dying*," Mira stammered. "You *have* to help me."

"No, I don't." The woman laced her age-spotted fingers together on the tabletop. "It's taken me quite a while to figure that out, my whole life in fact, but I don't *have* to do what's asked of me simply because it's expected." She narrowed her milky gaze at Mira. "I can choose."

<This lady's got no imagination. Dying and prison might not be much of a motivator, but I'll bet she still responds to pain.>

Mira nearly choked. *You want me to torture an old lady with barely a drop of magic in her veins? I'm not* that *much of a monster!*

<Do you see another option?>

Mira looked at Ty. A small crease puckered the space between his closed eyes, and a frown tugged the corners of his lips. One thing she'd learned in her time as his partner was that magic wasn't the solution to every problem. Ty's compassion had probably saved more people than Mira's magic. He'd saved her, monster though she was.

This woman is angry, Mira thought, *and who can blame her? We need to make her see that hurting the world that hurt her won't bring her the closure she's looking for.*

Sitting down across from the woman, Mira pressed her hands flat to the table and met that unsettling stare. "You're right. The choice *is* yours." She licked her lips, trying to work moisture into her dry mouth. "I understand feeling bitter about the hand you've been dealt, and I agree that you don't owe shit to your fae ancestor or the human authorities, but what about the innocent people this curse is hurting? What about the broke social worker who's watching his fiancé waste away in a hospital bed right how? What about the man who tried to stop his wife from burning herself and got carved up like a Christmas ham for his trouble? If you don't help me end this curse, how many more people are going to die?" She pointed at Ty. "Including him. Do you really want their blood on your hands?"

The woman shifted as if her seat had suddenly become uncomfortable, crossed her arms, and looked away, mumbling, "I didn't create this curse."

"But you *can* help me break it. You're my only lead to finding the person who cast the original enchantment."

The woman's laugh rustled like autumn leaves.

"Please," Mira said, "just tell me what you know."

"What I *know* is that the fae you're looking for doesn't care how many people die. Otherwise she'd be here already." The yellowed nail of the woman's pointer finger tapped scarred oak, stretching prominent tendons between the sagging flesh on the back of her hand. "In all honesty, I'd hoped the fae responsible for this situation would come to me if the coin killed enough people, drew enough attention. I wanted to look her in the face before I died and tell her that she'd ruined my life. Ruined my mother's life. Ruined my father's.

"Let me get this straight," Mira said, raising one hand. "You're using the curse as a billboard to call the fae who cast it in the first place?"

The woman pushed her silver hair behind her shoulder and nodded. "That creature cast a spell to punish thieves, but the ones she truly cursed were us, her supposed family."

"Supposed?" Mira asked.

"Related by blood, as you obviously knew when you got here, but not family by any other definition. She just needed a relative so far removed from her that no fae would think to look for her artifact among us. We were a parking space for her nasty little secret until she wanted it back. When she dumped the coin on my unwitting ancestor with a few basic instructions, she said she'd return for her treasure 'soon,' and that we were to keep it hidden until then, lest her enemies find us and kill us for it. I couldn't risk registering without either losing the coin or becoming a target. I've often considered chucking the damn thing off a bridge, but the fae was pretty clear about what would happen if she came back and we'd lost it."

Mira frowned. "How long has your family had the coin?"

She turned her face toward a window above the table, catching the last of the day's dying light on her wrinkled cheeks. "Seven generations."

The demon whistled. <So these poor schmucks have been saddled as guardians all that time, while the fae did as she pleased.>

Fae suck. Out loud, Mira said, "I'm sorry you and your family were used like that. I really am, but letting innocent people die won't change the past, and it won't punish the fae who did this to you."

The milky gaze swung over to Ty, assessing. "Who is he?"

Mira hesitated. "My partner. He found your coin on the previous victim during our investigation."

"Then I'm sorry, but your partner is going to die."

<The Rift he is.> The demon's presence stirred and swelled at the woman's pronouncement, and Mira felt her own protective emotions rising to match. Sparks danced over her skin as she struggled to keep their twin magics in check.

"That's not an option," Mira said through gritted teeth, smothering the light show tickling her knuckles.

The woman's mouth made a startled "o" at Mira's display.

Mira tensed. The demon roiled just under her skin. Their control had only slipped for a moment, but that was enough. They'd made a mistake.

This is why we can't afford to get emotionally attached, snarled the voice of fear in the echo chamber of Mira's mind. *Caring makes us sloppy.*

<We're definitely going to kill this lady, right?>

Mira compressed her lips. *The mistake was ours, not hers.*

<But she *saw* us.>

The woman's expression flickered between fear and curiosity—a dangerous combination—as she worked through possibilities. "Setting aside the foolhardy experiment in Colorado to train paranatural agents, the PTF doesn't let practitioners off their leashes, and fae aren't allowed to join." Her milky gaze narrowed. "So what are you?"

In for a penny, in for a pound.

"What I am," Mira said, letting the demon bleed through enough that her eyes momentarily shone gold and her hair turned white, "is dangerous and impatient."

The woman shrank slightly under Mira's threat, then she cleared her throat and straightened, lifting her chin. "Even if I wanted to save your friend, I can't. I don't know how."

"How can you keep a deadly weapon in your possession and not know how it works?" Mira demanded. "Obviously it hasn't killed *you.*"

"But it killed my father," she said in a dry rasp. "And don't you think I would have saved *him* if I'd known how?"

"It killed . . ." Mira couldn't finish the sentence. She was too busy watching the fragile wisps of her hope evaporate.

"When I was seven." The woman's voice took on a faraway quality at the memory. "We were living in Chicago back then. My mother kept the coin in her jewelry box, just as I did. She'd told me many times that it was very special, and I must never touch it, but she didn't tell me why. My father only knew that it was a family heirloom. He wasn't fae and, at the time, I didn't know I was either. I thought we were just a normal family with an heirloom coin." She stood up, crossed the room to a small kitchen area, and poured herself a glass of water from the sink. She didn't offer any to Mira, who waited with building dread for the rest of the story.

"My father wanted to do something special for my mother to celebrate their tenth anniversary. He decided to get the heirloom coin my mother was so fond of placed in a setting so she could wear it like the jewelry it lived beside. One day, while my mother was out, he took the coin, and the two of us went to a jeweler to commission the project. I told him he wasn't supposed to touch the coin, that Mama would be angry, but he assured me he was only borrowing it for a little while and promised Mama would be so happy to see what he'd done that she would forgive our taking it." She shrugged. "I was a child. I believed him."

After taking a long drink of water, she topped off her glass and returned to the table. "We left the coin with the jeweler and went out for ice cream. It was July. Hot and sunny. Papa kept complaining about the temperature. He bought more ice cream. Then he took off his shirt. Then he pushed behind the counter and tried to climb into the refrigerated display where the tubs of ice cream were kept."

<This sounds familiar.>

"The parlor owner pulled him out, and they fought. My father smashed the man's head against the display case hard enough to crack the glass, then he ran into the back of the building. People were screaming. Other employees. Customers. Kids. Me." She took another sip. "I followed him into the back while the adults called the police and tried to help the injured store owner. My father had locked himself in the walk-in freezer where the ice cream was kept. I was barely tall enough to see through the little window in the door, but he stripped off the rest of his clothes and started rubbing the ice cream all over his body like lotion. I tried to open the door, but he'd done something to jam it. Even when the adults tried later, they couldn't budge it. That door didn't open until the fire department sent a rescue crew. By the time they got him out, he was dead."

"I'm so sorry," Mira said.

The woman nodded, eyes moist with unshed tears. "I told my mother everything. She had me lead her to the jeweler whom my father had left her coin with and demanded it back. The jeweler gave it to her. He hadn't even started the project yet. My mom packed our belongings that very day, and we were on a bus before night fell. She said we weren't safe, that someone might notice what happened to my father and come looking for us." She shook her head, the tears finally falling. "Seven years old, and my whole world imploded in the course of one summer afternoon."

<I can see why she'd want to give the fae who cursed the coin a piece of her mind,> said the demon. <And maybe a good hook to the jaw.>

"That's when I found out I was part fae." The woman's voice grew stronger as she unburdened herself of this lifelong secret, perhaps placated by the fact the Mira clearly had secrets of her own. "This was all before the fae came out of hiding, of course, when magic was still a big secret in the human world. My mother told me what I was and all she knew about the curse that had killed my father. The coin supposedly belonged to a fae who had a great treasure here in the Mortal Realm sometime during the Middle Ages. After a human thief stole some of her treasure, she placed an enchantment on a golden coin to protect her remaining stash. Anyone who dared steal from her again would go mad with greed, killing themselves in pursuit of their obsession."

Mira's skin went cold, as if all the warmth had suddenly drained from the room. Then her brain snagged on a detail from the woman's story. "Golden?"

The woman nodded.

"The coin Ty touched was a quarter."

The woman frowned. "My coin was gold, stamped with a falcon on one side and a cross on the other."

<Maybe there's a glamour to make the coin blend in,> suggested the demon.

That would imply the fae wanted the coin to keep circulating after it was stolen.

<Makes sense.>

How so?

<If the coin looks harmless, it could take out not only the thief but the thief's family, their friends. It could wipe out a whole community before anyone figured out what was going on.>

Innocent people.

<Guilty by association. Fae are vindictive bastards as a rule, and crossing them comes at a steep price. Anyone connected to the thief would share in their debt; that makes them worth killing. Plus, it'd be easier for the fae to track the coin down if it's under a whole mountain of corpses rather than just one random human.>

I hate how much sense that makes to you.

<And I hate the way you clip your toenails, but it's practical.>

Mira waved a hand at the old woman. "Please, continue your story."

She frowned. "Mother wasn't sure why the fae eventually decided to hide the coin with her mortal relatives, or what happened to the rest of the fae's treasure, but she made it very clear that if any other fae found us, we'd be killed. If the humans discovered what we were, we'd be killed. And if we didn't have the coin when its owner returned, we'd be killed."

<Who would agree to a deal like that?> wondered the demon.

I don't think they were given much of a choice.

<Right. Probably something along the lines of, "Say no, and you'll be killed.">

"That first guardian passed down the coin and the warnings, descendant to descendant until it eventually came to my mother," continued the woman. "After my father died, Mom and I traveled from place to place, never staying long for fear that some fae or other would track us down to steal the coin. Mom worked whatever random jobs she could find. She took to drinking pretty heavily. What happened to my father . . . it broke her." She shook her head. "Eventually we landed at my grandparents' farm, having run out of money and options. My grandpa, from whom my mother inherited the coin, was gone by then, but Grandma kept the place running with a few hired hands. She had no idea what her husband had been, what my mother and I were." She sighed and rubbed one hand over her eyes.

Mira could relate. She'd run from her home, from her family, to hide what she was from them . . . to protect their normal world, their normal lives, from the chaos and danger of hers. Only fate had dragged her back, after a decade of isolation. Those wounds were still fresh, but they were finally starting to heal. From the sad look in the old woman's eyes, Mira didn't think she'd been granted that chance.

"My mother disappeared for a long time after that, lost to paranoia and alcohol. Then one night, when I was about fifteen, she snuck into my bedroom. She looked like a ghost and, at first, I thought she was one. She'd lost so much weight, and the only color in her skin was in the dark circles under her eyes. Then she wrapped my hands around her special coin and said, 'You're the guardian now.' I knew then that she was no spirit." A look of bitter resignation fell over the woman's weathered features like a shadow. "I never saw her again, and ever since that night, I've been a slave to that cursed coin . . . too afraid of what happened to my father, what might happen to anyone I dared get close to, to lead anything resembling a normal life."

Again the woman's words resonated deep within Mira. She looked around the tiny apartment with its bare walls and utilitarian furniture, noticing the single plate and fork on the drying rack by the sink. She thought of the makeshift home in the back of her truck, the people she met and left behind, the miles of road she'd covered on her journey to nowhere, and she shivered. *Is this my future? Alone? Wallowing in bitterness and regret?*

<You'll always have me,> said the demon. <Probably. Ultimately, *I'm* the one who'll end up alone, pulled back to the Rift when your meat suit gives out.>

"But I'm old now." The woman sounded tired. "And I'm the last of my line. If the fae doesn't come back for her coin, the curse will just go on killing people. I thought, if that happened before I died, I might at least meet her. Maybe find out why she did this to us."

Mira frowned, glancing again at Ty. He looked utterly vulnerable there on the woven rug where she'd deposited him. Thick cables of worry strangled her guts and squeezed her heart. Against her own advice, and despite the care she'd always taken not to get close to anyone—both for their protection and her own—she'd let Ty in. Not completely. Not yet. But she'd taken a step toward avoiding the regret and loneliness in this woman's clouded eyes.

This can't be the end of the breadcrumb trail, Mira insisted. *Not when Ty is still dying.*

The demon hovered at the back of Mira's mind, strangely subdued, which made Mira all the more frantic. She got the impression the demon felt as powerless at Ty's predicament as she did. Not a sensation either of them were used to.

"So you made a plan to lure the fae here, at the cost of innocent lives," Mira said, determined to keep the woman talking as she searched for any new thread to pull that might reveal a solution.

"Not at first. I'm not a psychopath. I didn't *plan* for anyone to die. Hell, I've spent my entire life trying to make sure that damned thing didn't get into the wrong hands. Well, anyone's hands. When I came home from my walk that day and saw the coin was gone, I was in a complete panic. I called the police right away and told them my jewelry had been stolen. I thought, if they were fast enough, maybe only the thief would die. But as days went by, I got to thinking that this might not be such a terrible thing after all. My mother always told me to keep a low profile, that if the fae noticed people dying in strange ways, they'd come to investigate the magic. I knew there was a risk the PTF would take notice, but this was my one shot at meeting the person who doomed my entire family."

<What if the wrong fae came looking?> asked the demon.

Mira repeated the question out loud.

"Then I'd ask them to contact the coin's owner." She shrugged. "Maybe they'd help me. Maybe they'd kill me. It really doesn't make a whole lot of difference at this point."

<Do you think Ms. Halfer here is right?> the demon wondered. <Will her fae show up if the body count climbs high enough?>

Mira's gaze settled once more on Ty, taking comfort from the steady rise and fall of his chest even as an invisible vise constricted her own. She hadn't known him for long, but even a few months was a record for her. She couldn't imagine going back to a world without him in it.

Even if her theory's sound, it doesn't matter. Focusing once more on the old woman, Mira said in a gruff voice that only shook a little, "I get that you want to draw the fae out with a body count so you can give her a piece of your mind, but Ty will *not* be one of those bodies." She slammed her fist on the table, wobbling a small blue vase of carnations and startling them both.

"I *am* sorry," the woman said. "If I could help you save him, I would, but I've told you everything I know."

"There must be *something*." Mira cast back through the woman's story, desperately sifting for any ray of hope. "What *exactly* did your mother say when she gave you the coin? She had to have a way of handing it off without cursing you."

Paper-thin eyelids closed over those clouded eyes. The woman tipped her head back, causing her silver mane to shimmer. "She said she gave the coin to me freely, and that my hands were the only ones in which the coin would be safe from that moment on."

"Okay," said Mira, "so you give the coin to Ty. Then he'll be the guardian, right? The curse will stop affecting him."

The old woman shook her head, eyes full of pity. "Only a person of the fae's bloodline can become a guardian. That's one of the rules."

<What about the jeweler?>

"What?" Mira was too agitated to pay attention to whether she was speaking out loud or not. "What about him?"

"What about who?" asked the old woman, looking confused. "Your friend?"

<Did the jeweler in her story die?> the demon clarified. <The one who gave the coin back?>

Mira jolted as though struck by lightning. She grabbed the woman's hands. "Did the jeweler who gave the coin back to your mother survive?"

The old woman recoiled from the sudden physical contact, but couldn't break Mira's grip. "Who knows?" This close the woman's breath smelled of peppermint and coffee. "We were gone by the next day." She shrugged. "I always assumed so."

"But you don't *know*?"

She shook her head.

"Then there's a chance!" Mira squeezed the woman's fingers, feeling her bones through the paper-thin skin, then she hurried over to Ty. Dropping to her knees beside him, she lifted his shoulders and cradled his head in her lap.

We need to give back enough energy to wake him up, but not enough for him to put up a fight if this doesn't work.

<Sure thing,> agreed the demon. <Are we doing this transfer the fun way?> Mira felt the demon's mischievous grin. <Or the boring way?>

Mira brushed her knuckles over Ty's cheek. Any skin-to-skin contact was enough for an energy transfer, but. . . . She glanced at the woman at the table—a woman who'd spent her entire life in fear, isolating herself from the world. And for what? To die alone in a shitty apartment, with no one to even notice when she's gone?

Squashing the familiar voice that insisted emotional complications would be the death of her, that "happily ever afters" weren't for monsters, Mira leaned down and pressed her lips to Ty's. Warm, soft, wet, she sank into the kiss as the first tendrils of energy drifted between them, tying their souls. In that moment, she allowed herself to pretend, to imagine they could be like this even when one of them wasn't dying, when there were no ulterior motives. Energy flowed like breath from Mira's lips to Ty's.

She savored the kiss, memorizing it. She'd kissed Ty before, but never by her own choice, only ever at the demon's impulse. This one felt different, more than just flesh meeting flesh—like a secret shared, or a wish granted.

A one-sided wish, she reminded herself, recalling Ty's use of the word "platonic" in the pawnshop. *An impossible wish . . . but a step in the right direction.*

The trickle of energy passing between them tapered off. Mira lingered for a moment, then straightened, tucking her fantasy away where it belonged. When she looked up, the old woman on whose rug she knelt was staring at her.

Those milky eyes darted from Mira to Ty, back to Mira. "I thought you were just coworkers?"

Heat crept into Mira's cheeks. "We are."

<Liar.>

One moonbeam eyebrow raised, seemingly in sync with the demon's comment, but the old woman said no more.

Ty groaned and stirred on Mira's lap.

<Just like Sleeping Beauty,> said the demon. <You woke him up with true love's kiss.>

The heat in Mira's cheeks intensified. She tucked a loose strand of hair behind her ear. *It was a practical decision.*

<Sure it was,> said the demon. <You didn't enjoy that at all.>

Unable to resist, Mira smiled down at Ty and whispered, "Rise and shine, Sleeping Beauty."

Chapter 10

Ty

TY GROANED. Every inch of him ached. His muscles felt like sandbags stitched into his skin. His legs and back were cold, but his shoulders rested on something lumpy and warm. He blinked his eyes open and was greeted by Mira's face in front of a popcorn-ceiling backdrop. Her cheeks were flushed with a rosy glow that made him want to touch them. She tucked the ever-present white strand of hair behind her ear and gifted him with a radiant smile.

"Rise and shine, Sleeping Beauty."

He blinked, trying to clear the cobwebs from his mind. Had he been asleep? The last thing he remembered clearly was sitting in the truck outside the apartment building where the woman who'd reported her jewelry stolen lived. He'd opened the door, then he'd hesitated. He only had one shoe on. How was a suspect supposed to take him seriously when he was only wearing one shoe?

Mira's face dimmed as all his focus swirled around that thought like matter being pulled into a black hole. He had to find a new shoe.

"How are you feeling?" Mira's voice pulled him back to the present, back to the apartment they were apparently in. Had Mira found the fae? Had she broken the curse?

No, he chided himself. *If she had, I wouldn't still be worrying about my damn shoe.* He cringed. Even the realization that he was still obsessing about shoes made him want to race to the nearest shoe store. He dug his nails into his palms. "I'm barely hanging on."

Mira's smile faltered. She lifted his shoulders, helping him to sit up, and he realized she'd been cradling him on her lap. "We've got a plan to fix you . . . hopefully."

"We?" His gaze settled on an elderly woman sitting at a beat-up table. She was silhouetted by dusk sky through a window behind her. "Is this . . .?"

"She's not the fae who cursed the coin," Mira said. Her voice carried an odd mixture of frustration and pity. "But she is the guardian of the coin. I'm hoping that the curse will nullify if you give the coin back to her."

"Then by all means." Ty reached for his pocket, remembering only when the cuffs caught that his hands were bound together. Moving both arms, he dug awkwardly in the pocket where he'd tucked the coin until his fingers closed around the evidence bag with its solitary occupant. He tore off the plastic. The coin was heavy on his palm. It looked like an ordinary quarter, but it had a gravity to it that weighed him down and stole his concentration.

Mira cleared her throat. He glanced up, and she tipped her chin toward the old woman. Ty tucked his legs and got to his knees. Every motion was an effort. He felt as if he were recovering from a week of flu. Climbing laboriously to his feet, he took three steps across the apartment, noting the rustic furniture and simple decorations. Approaching the woman, who glared at him as though he held a poisonous snake, he wracked his memory for the name from the police report.

"Ms. Bransen," he said with a rasp like a lifetime smoker. "I believe this belongs to you." He offered the coin, pleased that his hands didn't appear to shake despite how wobbly he felt.

Ms. Bransen pursed her lips and stared daggers at the coin on his palm. Her gaze, clouded by cataracts, flitted to Mira then back to the coin. She frowned, sighed heavily, then plucked the coin from his hand, pinching it between two fingers as though loath to touch it.

Ty's knees wobbled. He sat heavily on the second chair and took a deep breath.

"How do you feel?" Mira's warm hand squeezed his shoulder.

He reached up to cover her fingers with his, inhaled, and looked down at his sock-clad foot. The once-white sock was a sickly grayish color and crusted with dirt. An overwhelming panic flared within him. *This is totally unacceptable. I have to find a replacement right away!*

He started to rise, but Mira's firm grip pushed him back into his seat with hardly any effort at all. Ty was already panting.

"Ty?"

He stared into her mismatched eyes, trying to find the words that would convey his deep need, finally settling for the woefully inadequate, "I need new shoes."

Disappointment washed over Mira's expression. She gave his shoulder another squeeze. "Soon." She reached in her own pocket, pulled something out, and wrapped Ty's hands around a smooth, solid weight. "Focus on this until then."

Turning to the older woman, Mira said, "It didn't work."

Ms. Bransen shrugged. "It was a long shot. For all we know that jeweler died as soon as my mother and I left the store."

Curiosity warred with compulsion in Ty's mind. He opened his hands and ran his thumb over the river rock he carried as an anchor. Why had Mira had it? Closing his eyes, he traced the stone's curves, the single gash across its surface. His breathing slowed. His thoughts stilled. He opened his eyes and focused on Mira. "What jeweler?"

Mira related the story of how Ms. Bransen's father had died from the same curse that was now threatening Ty, and she told him about the jeweler from whom her mother had retrieved the coin. "I thought maybe, since he gave it back, the curse might not have killed him," Mira said.

"Did you check?" Ty asked.

Mira tipped her head toward the old woman. "She didn't know. She was seven, and they left Chicago right after her mom got the coin back."

"Do you remember the name of the store?" he asked Ms. Bransen. "Or even the street it was on?"

She pursed her lips. "It was all so long ago . . ."

Reaching once more into his pocket, Ty retrieved his phone, noting for the first time that his badge was missing. Frowning, he looked at Mira. "Do you know what happened to my badge?"

Cheeks flushing in that adorable way, she handed over the leather case that held his PTF ID. "I had to borrow it."

Ty arched an eyebrow. "You can explain later."

Ms. Bransen watched the exchange as if Ty and Mira were characters on some TV drama.

Tucking the badge away, Ty opened a map on his phone and zoomed in on Chicago. He set the phone on the table, facing Ms. Bransen. "Can you remember the route you took with your father that day?"

Ms. Bransen studied the map, zooming in and out to identify landmarks. She pointed to the screen. "This should be the park that was next to our apartment." She scrolled down and to the right. "This is the plaza where we went for ice cream." Her voice tightened on the words "ice cream," and Ty wondered if the treat had been forever ruined for the seven-year-old in Mira's story. She zoomed in again, studying the streets. "The jewelry store had to be in this block here." She indicated a wide avenue.

A few keyword searches led Ty to *Marwan Jewelry*—family owned and operated since 1943.

"That's it," Ms. Bransen shouted, eyes wide. "Mr. Marwan. That was the man my father spoke with."

Ty found a phone number for the store and dialed.

"Marwan Jewelry, how can I help you?" said a cheerful-sounding woman.

"My name is Ty Williams," said Ty. "I'm a PTF agent, and I have a few questions about the man who ran your store about seventy years ago."

"That would have been my grandfather, Amir Marwan. What's this about?"

"Can you tell me how your grandfather died?" Ty asked.

"Old age," the woman said, sounding confused. "He died in bed when he was eighty-two."

"How long ago was that?"

"I was in high school, so . . . about twenty years ago, I guess."

Hope bubbled up. Ty tried to keep his excitement out of his voice as he asked, "Are you aware of any strange deaths that happened during your grandfather's time running the store? Perhaps an employee who died under unusual circumstances?"

"No dead employees that I know of, but Grandpa told me a story once about a *customer* who went crazy. I guess he locked himself in a freezer. Does that help?"

Ty took a shuddering breath, as if straps that had been constricting his chest all day had suddenly loosened. "Yes." His voice shook with relief. "Yes, that helps. Thank you so much."

"Um, sure. Have a nice day." The woman hung up, and Ty put his phone away.

He smiled at Mira. "That jeweler lived for forty years after touching the coin."

"The curse kills within two days," said Ms. Bransen.

"Then it *is* possible to remove the curse." Mira frowned at Ms. Bransen. "You must have missed something that your mother did to the jeweler when she took the coin back."

"Probably." Ms. Bransen scowled. "I was seven years old, and I'd just watched my father kill himself. I wasn't exactly paying attention."

"This is important," Mira took a step toward Ms. Bransen, fists balled. "You need to remember what your mother did when she took the coin back."

Ms. Bransen bristled.

Ty raised a shaky hand, drawing the attention of the two agitated women. "Everybody, calm down."

Why would they listen to me? I look like a vagrant. I need . . . I need . . . He tightened his grip on the stone in his other hand as he felt the impulse to run from the room rise up. *Stay in the moment!*

"Ty? Ty!" Mira's worried expression hovered inches from his face. "Are you all right?"

He met her gaze and swallowed past the painful tightness in his throat. His thoughts were fraying. It was getting harder and harder to think about anything except—*No!* He dragged his focus back to Mira. "Let me try something."

Mira frowned, but nodded and moved away.

"Try what?" asked Ms. Bransen, her eyes narrowed in suspicion. "I've already told your angry girlfriend everything I remember."

Ty smiled, though it felt strained. "Let's start over, Ms. Bransen. My name is Ty Williams. I'm a PTF field agent. I apologize for any unpleasantness I may have caused you earlier. I haven't been entirely myself since touching that coin."

Ms. Bransen seemed to deflate like a bird settling its feathers. She twitched her chin toward Mira, who'd started pacing around the room. "What's her excuse?"

Ty chuckled and said, "People skills are still somewhere on her to-do list."

Mira crossed her arms, grumbled something under her breath, and pivoted to start another circuit.

Ty and Ms. Bransen exchanged grins, then her smile faded. "She's worried about you, and for good reason." She shook her head. "I'm sorry. You seem like a nice man."

"Thanks," Ty said, "but I'm not dead yet. At least one person who touched the coin seems to have survived this curse. It *is* possible."

"You'd think your mom would have given you a manual or something," Mira grumbled. "Who hands their kid a loaded gun and doesn't tell them where the safety is?"

Ms. Bransen frowned.

Ty waved Mira away. "Don't mind her. Let's talk about you. It must have been hard, all those years, not being able to talk to anyone about this burden you were hiding."

"It was . . . isolating," she admitted. "I was glad Mom got us out of Chicago, at least. I couldn't have borne going back to school, seeing the neighbors, knowing my father was branded a crazy person, and not being allowed to set the record straight."

He nodded. "I imagine you've buried your memories of that time, maybe even tried to forget them. It's only natural. None of us like to recall painful moments from our past." Clutching his anchor stone in one hand to keep the constant scraping in his mind at bay, he set the fingers of his free hand against the papery skin of Ms. Bransen's wrist, scraping his handcuffs against the table. "If you're willing, I'd really appreciate if you'd try to recreate that day with me."

Ms. Bransen stared into his eyes for a moment, shot a glance at Mira pacing a hole through her floor, and exhaled. "I can't promise anything, but I'll try."

"That's all anyone can ever do." Ty gave her an encouraging smile. "Let's start with when your father dropped the coin off. What did you notice about the jewelry store?"

Ms. Bransen closed her eyes. "It was . . . clean. There were glass cases with jewelry displays. My father told me not to touch anything." The corner of her mouth quirked up. "I remember pointing out a little silver ballerina charm. It had pink shoes and a diamond for a head."

"Sounds lovely," Ty said. "Did you do ballet?"

"No," she said quietly, "but I always wanted to."

"Can you picture the person working behind the counter?" Ty asked.

Ms. Bransen nodded, sending a shimmer of silver hair cascading over her shoulder. "He was tall. Heavy. With brown skin. He had a big, flat nose and a dark beard that covered the whole bottom half of his face." She scrunched her nose in concentration. "He wore glasses, and he smiled a lot. Especially when Dad shook his hand."

"He must have spoken to your father. Can you recall his voice?"

The pucker between Ms. Bransen's eyebrows grew more pronounced. "He had a deep voice."

"What did he say to your father?"

"He said the project would be no problem. It would be done the next day."

Ty licked his lips, closing in on the gold at the end of the rainbow. "Later, you heard the man speak again, this time to your mother."

Ms. Bransen's fingers curled against the oak table.

"It's okay," Ty said. "You must have been very upset at that point."

"I was crying," she confirmed. "Mama was furious. I was afraid she blamed me for what happened to my father."

"But it wasn't your fault," Ty said. "She was probably angry with herself, and maybe a little afraid for the man in the store. The man with the big nose and deep voice. Did she talk to him?"

Ms. Bransen nodded. "She yelled at him."

"What did she yell?" Ty prompted.

"That he had to give her coin back; it was hers, and Papa had no right giving it to the jeweler." She swallowed. "The man didn't smile at Mama the way he had when he spoke to my father. He looked upset."

"Yelling moms have that effect," Ty said. "Did he agree to give back the coin?"

"Yes . . ." Ms. Bransen frowned. "But that wasn't enough. Mama said he had to apologize."

"What for?" Mira's voice broke into the intimacy of their conversation.

Ty shot her a glare, then focused again on Ms. Bransen, who still had her eyes closed.

"He argued," she said. "He didn't seem to understand why my mother wouldn't take the coin back without an apology. It made him angry. His cheeks turned purple. But Mama insisted. I think he finally gave in just to get her out of the store before he lost his temper completely."

Ty squeezed Ms. Bransen's arm lightly. "Focus on the man. When he handed back the coin, what did he say?"

Ms. Bransen's expression pinched, then her eyes snapped open. "That's *it!*" she said breathlessly.

Dislodging Ty's grip with a shake of her wrist, she pressed the cursed coin into his hand. Her mouth was a tight line of concentration, but her eyes were full of hope when they met his. "Repeat after me." She cleared her throat. "I return this treasure to its rightful hand and beg forgiveness for my transgression."

Mira came closer, hovering near his shoulder.

Ty repeated the phrase word for word.

Ms. Bransen opened her hand, and Ty set the quarter on her palm.

The coin seemed to shimmer. A ripple cascaded across the surface of the metal and, in its wake, silver turned to gold. The wigged head of George Washington became a stylized cross.

Mira gave a little squeak and clapped her hands. She grabbed Ty's shoulders and stared into his eyes. "Well?"

Leaning past her, Ty stared at his gray sock. He wiggled his toes. The sock was disgustingly dirty. Unsalvageable. He would definitely need to buy a new pair of shoes . . . but not right now. Gently pushing Mira away, he yanked off his remaining shoe, stared at it for a moment, then tossed it aside. "I think I'll go barefoot for a while."

Mira dropped onto her butt with a heavy exhale, shaking her head. "I swear, you are going to be the death of me." She glanced at Ms. Bransen. "Thanks."

"It's amazing how much better a person's memory works when they're not being yelled at or threatened."

Mira rolled her eyes. "Yeah, yeah. I suck at people. We know."

"I *am* grateful," Ty said, drawing Ms. Bransen's attention. "You saved my life."

"Do you think the gas station clerk has to apologize separately?" Mira asked. "Or was that, like, a blanket anti-curse?"

Ms. Bransen shrugged. "I have no idea."

Ty stood, offered Mira a hand, and pulled her to her feet, swaying slightly on his own. Dizziness made him sit back down. "Why don't you head over to the hospital and check on Matthew while I discuss next steps with Ms. Bransen?"

Mira nodded and pulled a small, silver key out of her pocket. "Ready to take those bracelets off?"

"Yes, please." Ty offered his wrists.

Mira unlocked both cuffs. Energy surged into Ty as she trailed her fingers over his, lingering for a moment at the tips. She stepped back with a smile.

He shivered, feeling electrified, relieved, and yet somehow exhausted, all at the same time. "Thanks."

"Don't mention it." She set the cuffs and key on the table and headed for the door, but she stopped with her hand on the doorknob. "I've got an acquaintance at the PTF who happens to be related to a big shot in the fae Court of Enchantment." Mira kept her back to the room, as if she were conversing with the door. "I can't make any promises, but they might be able to track down the coin's original owner."

Ms. Bransen stiffened then said, "I would appreciate that."

Ty looked back and forth between the two women, totally lost. The curse was broken. Why were they still looking for the original owner?

Mira open the door and slipped out without so much as a goodbye.

"Sorry," he said to Ms. Bransen. "She really does need to work on her people skills."

"I don't know." Ms. Bransen wiped a tear from her cheek. "Maybe she's not so bad."

RAIN PATTERED upon the wide umbrella, dripping from its edges in a glittering curtain that cocooned Ty and Mira, separating them from the other funeral attendees. Ty tried to pay attention to what the priest at the graveside was saying, but he kept getting distracted by warm touches and the scent of lavender soap as Mira bumped against his side under their shared cover. The two of them stood at the back of a crowd of Agent Reyes's family, friends, and coworkers, each in their own protective bubbles, as the ground turned into a swamp beneath their feet and the priest droned on about duty and sacrifice.

Ty stared at the dark wood that held Agent Reyes's body and tried not to think about how easily it could have been him in that box. He'd survived. As had Matthew Clark, though verifying the gas station attendant had been released from his compulsion hadn't been as simple as a quick trip to the hospital. The staff had been unwilling to bring him out of sedation until his surgery was complete. Still, that had given Mira somewhere to be while Ty arranged the safe storage and transport of the cursed coin and dealt with all the corresponding paperwork of the case, including a rather embarrassing explanation and apology regarding his behavior in the airport hangar.

Water droplets rolled off the oiled surface of Reyes's casket, preceding him into the muddy hole as the box began its descent. The priest finished his prayer and bowed his head. Mira did likewise, one hand closed around the saint medallion hanging from her neck.

Ty shifted his feet, squelching mud under the Walmart sneakers Mira had bought him three days before so he wouldn't have to walk out of Ms. Bransen's apartment barefoot. They weren't up to his usual standards, but they fit . . . and that was enough. He'd considered buying something more appropriate for the funeral, but the thought of setting foot in a shoe store had soured his stomach. He took a deep breath, the air rich with the smells of rain and tilled earth, and savored the fact that he didn't care at all that he was standing in wet socks and neon-yellow sneakers caked with mud.

The priest said, "Amen," and the crowd came alive. Some people moved closer to the grave, tossing white roses into the hole. Some headed straight for a nearby tent to get out of the rain. A few, likely Reyes's family, remained huddled in a tight cluster at the graveside. Ty's heart lurched as the scene was overlain by memories of another funeral. Reyes's family morphed in his imagination, taking on the features of his own. The sky had been clear and blue that day, mocking his sadness. His guilt. He shook his head and bumped Mira with his elbow, saying gruffly, "Let's leave them to their grief."

She looked up, meeting his gaze with an unsure expression, as if she wanted to say something but couldn't decide what. She bit her lower lip, drawing his attention to the crimson bow of her mouth. A warmth he had no intention of acknowledging stirred deep inside him.

Clearing his throat, he turned toward the parking lot, forcing her to join him or lose the shelter of the umbrella.

"Agent Williams!" Kelley's voice jerked Ty to a stop. The young agent wore a clear poncho that clung to his dark suit. Mud splashed his boots and the hem of his pants as he trotted over. "Thanks for coming," he said, planting himself directly in their path, "and for solving the case. Now Reyes can rest in peace." He glanced over Ty's shoulder, toward the grave. "I only wish I could have helped more."

"You were plenty helpful," Mira said. "It was great to have someone doing research for us, so we could focus on the ground work."

"Yeah," Kelley said. "I guess. I just feel like . . . I don't know." He hung his head.

Ty reached out and set a heavy hand on the younger man's wet, plastic-covered shoulder, ignoring the raindrops that dampened his sleeve. "You feel responsible," Ty said knowingly.

Kelley met his gaze with a lost expression, like a kid looking for comfort.

"You aren't." Ty squeezed. "The loss of a partner is . . ." His throat constricted. "You won't ever get over it, but you *can* move past it. And you have to. You're a good agent. Someday you'll be a great one. Keep moving forward, or the weight of regret will stop you in your tracks."

Mira shot him a knowing look. He tilted his face away to avoid eye contact.

Kelley swiped a hand through his damp hair, snagging on the poncho's hood. "I still can't believe so many lives were ruined by an inanimate object." He gave Ty a sharp look. "You're sure it can't curse anyone else?"

"Not unless someone were to break into the secure PTF vault and pry open the welded iron box we put it in."

"Right," Kelley said. "I'm sure it's fine. The PTF stores lots of dangerous artifacts." He shook his head. "I just wish we knew where it came from."

Ty nodded in commiseration, noting that Mira chose that moment to examine her shoes. They'd agreed that Ms. Bransen deserved to live what remained of her life on her own terms, not prosecuted by the PTF for housing an illegal artifact. She'd spent most of her life trying to keep people safe from her family's magic trinket. That had to be punishment enough. Mira had also sent word to her acquaintance—whose name she refused to share with Ty—and started the wheels turning to track down the coin's creator on Ms. Bransen's behalf. Now *that* was someone Ty wouldn't mind arresting.

"There will always be mysteries," Ty said to Kelley. "Comes with the territory. Just deal with what's in front of you, and remember to celebrate your victories, however incomplete they may feel."

Kelley shook Ty's hand. "Yeah. Thanks again." He offered his hand to Mira. "You two make a good team. You should consider joining the PTF as a full agent, instead of just a consultant."

Mira smiled, but Ty caught the pinch around her eyes that showed it was forced. "I'll think about it." She gave Kelley's hand a stiff shake.

Kelley nodded once then jogged away to join the remaining attendees under the tent, where they would share stories about Agent Reyes and celebrate his life. Ty hadn't made it to the reception after Jamal's funeral. He hadn't even made it through the service. He shivered under the remembered stares of his friends and family. Logically he knew he must have imagined the accusation in those eyes, but he couldn't shake the feeling that they blamed him. Jamal had been more than a partner; he'd been a brother, and Ty's choice had killed him.

"He's a good kid," Mira's voice jarred Ty out of his memory. She was staring after Kelley with a mixture of pity and envy as the group of grievers welcomed him into their ranks with open arms. "He's got people to help him through. He'll be okay." She glanced up at Ty, and he wasn't quick enough this time to avoid getting caught by the pull of her mismatched eyes. "For a while there, when you were cursed, I really thought . . ." Her brow crinkled, and she looked away.

"You thought I wouldn't survive," Ty finished.

She nodded, staring at the fresh grave. "I've never had a partner I could lose before," she said quietly. "But now . . . I think I understand why Jamal's death haunts you."

Ty followed her gaze, feeling the slow roil of emotions spread in tingling numbness through his body. He felt like a hypocrite for telling Kelley to move forward when he himself had been trapped in quicksand ever since he ran from Jamal's funeral. He'd agreed to take up his badge again after meeting Mira, but it would be a lie to say that he'd actually moved past Jamal's death. He couldn't truly do that until he got up the nerve to face the people he'd let down—both Jamal's family and his own. He wasn't sure he'd ever be ready for that, but neither could he hide from them forever.

"We should celebrate the fact that we're both still alive," Mira said with a mischievous grin, short-circuiting his spiraling thoughts, as she so often did. "How about a new pair of shoes?"

Ty groaned, letting himself be dragged toward the truck. "How about dinner? My treat."

Want more?
Continue the adventure with
Dancing with a Demon
Book 4 of the Rifter series.

Acknowledgments

I hope you enjoyed reading this Rifter novella. I certainly enjoyed writing it!

It was fun to play with a different story length.

First and foremost, I'd like to thank my editor, Debra Dixon, for agreeing to publish a shorter-length work and, as always, providing invaluable advice and guidance throughout the process. I also owe a lot to my loyal alpha and beta readers, who don't grumble even when I give them tight turn-around times. And I want to thank my family and friends for their continued support and encouragement.

More than anyone, though, I want to thank YOU, for taking this detour with me. I love spending time with Mira and Ty, and I hope you'll continue to read their adventures!

About the Author

L.R. Braden is a bestselling, multi-award-winning author of dark-yet-hopeful urban fantasy stories. Her published works include the *Magicsmith* series, the *Rifter* series, and several works of shorter fiction. A bit of a recluse, she enjoys collecting skills that may (or may not) prove useful in the event that she is suddenly transported to an inhospitable alternate reality. Since that hasn't happened yet, she mostly spends her days weaving fantastic tales, playing with her family, and getting lost on purpose. Her writing has won many awards, including the Eric Hoffer Book Award for Sci-fi/Fantasy, the Next Generation Indie Book Award for Paranormal Fiction, and the Imadjinn Award for Best Urban Fantasy.

Connect with her online at lrbraden.com